Deception and Damage

Adventures of a Villain-Leaning Humanoid

Book Four

Jamie Jackson

Editor: Mary Beth Foster

Cover Art: Reilly Jackson

CONTENT/TRIGGER WARNINGS

Psychic/mental coercion, blood & gore, harsh language, sex and sexual situations, sexual assault, misgendering, pregnancy

CONTENTS

ACKNOWLEDGMENTS

Thank you to my husband and children, who once again have supported me even through all their "complaints".

Thank you to Jennifer, who continues to put up with my incessant cliff-hanger texting about these stories.

CHAPTER ONE

You know eventually you're going to remember my name, right? Megaera, but no one calls me that, just Meg.

Last time you came around we met Ares, about twenty different giant-ass snakes, and a Medusa. Medusus? I don't know, Ares says they didn't get the name right anyway, so it could be something completely different. Well, if you paid attention, maybe you would remember the exact number of snakes involved. Another hero joined our team, a fire starter named Maniac.

I'm forgetting something. That's right – Poseidon forced a servitude debt on me and then acted like it was all cool.

Oh, and Hera showed up last minute to give me her blessing, which wasn't ominous at all.

The most important part, though, was Greg made Virgil drive us all over to the courthouse as soon as we got back from Ranger's team building exercise of camping. Yep, we're married now. Sorry you weren't invited. Don't feel bad about it. Greg's family wasn't either.

All caught up?

Let's get going.

∞

I knew something weird had to be going on when I got up and headed over to the kitchen because the smell of the eggs Greg was cooking made me gag. Look, I've got a sensitive nose, but not that sensitive.

And the last couple nights when we were cuddling on the couch watching musicals – yes, I finally got him to watch musicals with me – I've started falling asleep halfway through. It's not even that late, like, we're talking maybe nine or ten at night, and we're both used to having to work much later nights.

What really clinched it was when I went to drink my coffee and my stomach immediately rolled over.

Oh, hell no. I better not be sick.

"Something wrong?" Greg asked. His blonde hair had flopped into his face, hanging in the way of his dark brown eyes. He was still shirtless, and normally I totally would've taken the opportunity to watch the flex of his muscles as he moved – physically as strong and imposing as his hero name, Fortress, implied.

"My stomach is off," I said. "I think I picked up some kind of bug."

Greg looked like he was about to say something, but there was a knock at the door. "It's open," he called. Virgil swung the door open and had barely come in before he was giving me that long, considering look he does. He wasn't wearing his duster, the abstract sleeve tattoos on his arms exposed, one hand up at his chin, fingers resting against his dark brown beard – wiry and lean muscle to Greg's broad shoulders.

Heroes have a thing for clingy t-shirts, it seems.

"You okay, Meg?" Virgil asked.

"Fine, just a stomach bug," I said, trying to ignore the queasiness. It wasn't working.

"Hmm," he said. "There should be things for nausea in the medical supply closet in the lab. Go take a look. Greg, if I can see you down in security?" Greg set aside the pan of eggs, following Virgil out the door. I went along in their wake and down the stairs to the floor below us. The lab was closer, so while they headed down the hallway on Virgil's floor, I went through the clearly marked laboratory door.

Oh yeah, we also got to move into our actual headquarters. They were finished after we got done fighting all the giant snakes. We moved in a couple weeks after we got back from camping (never underestimate the motivation a telekinetic has when it comes to his pet projects). Pretty sure Virgil was coming over getting drywall and things done just so that the space would be ready sooner. We moved in, what, five or so weeks ago?

The two weeks between camping and moving we spent in a hotel. A cheap one, in a bad part of town that drove Greg nuts safety wise, but Virgil convinced him it would be fine because no one would think to look for us there, so we wouldn't need to worry about any of the other villains hunting down Maniac.

This won't surprise you, but Virgil is super organized. He even has the medical supply closet labeled, and he was not kidding about there being supplies. The "closet" took up half the room. There was shelving all against the walls and installed up and down the width of the space. He even had signs marking where the different things were. It was like he had lifted up a pharmacy and plopped it into the room.

I went straight for the sign that said *over the counter.*

He stocked everything, and I mean everything. Tylenol, Midol, Dayquil, Pepto-Bismol, Benadryl, a plethora of vitamins – if any of us got sick with something that wasn't villain-inflicted, Virgil had the cure for what ails us.

He even had a stack of single-packaged pregnancy tests.

Wait, why did he even have those?

I paused my perusal. Well, Maniac and Ranger had been shacking up since we had taken out the Gorgon. Which, as far as I'm concerned, yeah, get it girl! I don't know what their prevention methods are, but I'm pretty sure Greg and I are safe because, IUD.

Oh no, I have been religious about that. It's one of the few things I act like a responsible adult on because I do not need to be inflicting myself on a baby. Basically, as soon as my parents kicked me out and I got set up with a job and could support myself, that was one of the first things I set aside money for. No health insurance at the time, and they wouldn't have covered it anyway, assholes. And I made sure to keep up with when it would need to be replaced.

If you remember anything about the first time we met, I told you, a girl has needs. Greg wasn't the first. Even with protection on the other person's end, I wasn't taking chances. I do stupid things but not that stupid.

Actually, Greg and I have continued to double up on the protection with condoms every time.

I was still staring at the tests, though, thinking. When was my last period? The thought slid in, out of focus, misting away as I tried to catch why I hadn't missed it sooner. The last one I could remember was before we went camping, which was super inconvenient because of the giant snakes at the time. And that was almost three months ago.

Oh, fuck. The shore of the lake. When Greg came out of the tent. He hadn't brought any protection with him, and at the time, it hadn't even occurred to me. Which left a different question – why hadn't either of us hit the pause button like we always did?

That bitch did not. Hera better not have. I will tear her eyes out, rip her God damn skin off and wear it if she did.

Could a goddess and her so called blessing defeat modern tech? Because I wouldn't put it past her to try this as a deterrent for Zeus.

I slipped one of the pregnancy tests up my sleeve.

Yes, I have long sleeve shirts now. I had to get some. I've got to cover up that ridiculous catsuit somehow, and Greg's got a problem with me risking all his sweatshirts for some reason.

I poked my head out of the lab, listening, ears straining. I didn't want to go down to security to check and see if Greg and Virgil were still there. I wanted to haul my ass back upstairs and make sure in secret that I was overreacting because I wasn't sure what Greg's reaction would be.

Look, between the villains, monsters and now gods, we haven't had much time to discuss how we feel about kids. And yeah, I know, kind of important to talk about with a person *before* you get married, but I had assumed what with our jobs and not wanting to endanger people around us, kids might not be on the table at all. Certainly not at this point in time.

Look, I don't talk about the important shit. I just kind of hedge around it and pretend it doesn't exist until someone else confronts me with it, so I had let the whole kid discussion lie. Greg seems like the type to want kids, but from his overall "can't go settle down and raise a family because of my hero job" attitude, I had also kind of taken it for granted he came to the conclusion they weren't in the cards for him.

I didn't even know if I wanted kids. I had always just assumed they weren't going to be an option for me anyway, considering what I've done in the past, so I never really thought about whether I would maybe one day have any. The whole head in the sand kind of thing. What kind of parent could I possibly be? A shitty one, most likely.

The whispers were curling over my shoulders, and I waved them off. I needed to focus, and I was getting distracted. I could hear Greg and Virgil's voices down the hallway, so I picked my way back over to the stairs, snuck through the door and then hightailed it up the stairs.

Once I got back into our apartment and over to the bathroom, I dithered over whether to lock it. I never lock it; Greg knows I don't lock it. If I locked it, he would know something was up.

Damn it. I locked it anyway. I slipped the box out of my sleeve, tore it open and read the instructions. Five minutes?! It was going to take five minutes? I didn't know if I had that kind of time.

Muttering to myself, I got the test itself unwrapped and got down to business. Do you have any idea how hard it is to pee on a stick and not get pee on your own hand? How short do these tests need to be anyway? I set it on the counter, instructions in one hand, impatiently glancing back and forth between the two. I was overreacting, right? I had to be overreacting.

One pink line appeared. Okay, that was the control line, so I just needed to be patient and there'd be nothing else—

Oh.

Oh no.

That was not five fucking minutes!

Two very bright pink lines were staring up at me. I reread the instructions. Maybe I did something wrong? But the instructions were short and clear. Two lines equals pregnant.

I couldn't tell if I wanted to laugh or cry in that moment, scream or shout. Can you do both at the same time? Whatever emotions I had churning in there definitely included an edge of panic.

The whispers were there, murmuring in my ears, strangely reassuring, calm and serene as they, the figures and shadows curled around me. I took a breath. If they were managing not to destroy things in the bathroom in response to my current state, I could calm the fuck down too.

They faded once my breathing had returned to something somewhat normal.

I needed to think. I would have to call my doctor. I hadn't found a new one closer to the center of the city, so I was going to need to head back out to the outskirts where I used to live. I couldn't leave the IUD in. I had to find out how far along I was.

I would have to tell Greg. Eventually there would be a second heartbeat (When does that heartbeat even start? I didn't know the first thing about how this worked), and he would hear it. Even if I wanted, and tried, to hide it from him, I would fail. We live together; there's no way he would miss that kind of change. What was I going to do? Spend nine months wearing increasingly baggy clothes and refusing to be naked around him? Not suspicious at all.

And what about when there's a baby here? He'd have to be a special kind of dumb to not notice an entire person in the apartment. Small as that person would be at first.

Where would the baby sleep? We have a studio. I couldn't put a baby up in the loft, and definitely not in the panic room.

Who would the baby look like? Would they have my black curls? Greg's brown eyes or my grey? My olive-toned, always-tanned skin?

I realized I was making plans to keep it. Keep him, or her. It made me pause. There was another option here, wasn't there? But the thought felt blocked, sluggish, hidden behind a wall I couldn't dig or move past. Thick and insubstantial at the same time, I couldn't pin down what or why it was wrong.

A knock at the bathroom door made me jump, the realization slipping away. "Just a second!" I yelled.

"Are you alright?" Greg. Shit. I hadn't figured out how to tell him yet. I had been too busy staring at the damn test.

"Fine," I squeaked, my heart hammering again, because what would he say?

A pause on the other side. Then, warily. "You don't sound fine. Why is the door locked?"

I snatched the test and instructions up, opened the door, shoved them both into Greg's hands, and slammed the door shut in his startled face and leaned against it. It was the best I could do without locking it again.

I'm nothing if not adorable about this kind of thing. Cutest way to tell someone ever, right?

There was silence on the other side. The crinkle of crumpled paper. What do they print those instructions on? Because they're loud. Silence again.

"Meg?" His voice was hoarse. "Meg, will you open the

7

door please?"

I got off the door and cracked it open. "Hi."

"Hi," he said. He was smiling. I had never seen him smile with that kind of joy.

Okay, I lied. He smiled like that the first time he told me he loved me and he heard the way my heart sped up. His eyes had lit up the same way then, too.

But this time was different because he looked like he was on the verge of tears at the same time.

"Can you come out of the bathroom?" he asked me.

I pulled the door open and slid out, standing in front of him, trying – and failing – not to keep looking down at the floor. Because what if he didn't want him or her?

"Meg," he said. "Look at me. Does this – is this – is this what I think it is?" He was holding the test and instructions out at me. His hands were shaking.

"Yes," I whispered. The volume didn't matter; I knew he would hear me.

"Are you—" he couldn't seem to finish the words. "Are you?" he repeated.

"Yes."

He laughed, snatched me up and spun me. And then his lips were pressed against mine, his hand in my hair. He set me down, one arm wrapped around me, lips still on mine, then my neck, his breath in my ear, back to my lips. He pulled back, grinning at me.

In that moment, he sobered, the grin slowly fading from his face. "Are you okay with this?"

I had to take a breath because the panic had spiked again, and I was on another precipice, another choice before me. His eyes were searching mine.

If I lied, he would hear it in the beat of my heart. But the thought of choosing anything else slid away. In that moment, the certainty bloomed upward, unfolding like the petals of a lily, that this choice was unquestionable.

"Yes," I said.

"A baby," he said, one hand pressed gently against my stomach.

I cleared my throat. "Yup. A baby." The panic was slowly fading. I would probably panic again later.

I was still going to tear Hera's fucking eyes out.

"Our baby," he said. He kissed me again.

Okay, the eyeball tearing and skin-wearing vengeance could wait a while.

∞

"We're going to have to tell my mom," he said while we were cuddled on the couch later.

"Do we have to?" I asked. When we had told her we were engaged she hadn't responded well. And his brothers had gone off tattling to his dad, who had actually been pleased with the turn of events.

He and Greg were slowly building a relationship, but it was rough going. Apparently, Flightpath had put a lot of blame on his ex-wife for never understanding the whole hero part, and Greg wasn't having it. He was fiercely loyal to her, even when I thought he might want to take a step back from the situation and try a different lens. I think he chose to continue blaming Flightpath for leaving and never seeing him, even when his own mom had a hand in that. Greg seemed to think his dad should've tried harder and that his mom's intentions were only to protect him.

He would be the type to see it that way.

He chuckled. "Yeah, we have to." Then he straightened up. "We have to tell Virgil."

"Well, yeah, I think he would notice eventually—" I started.

"No, Meg, I mean right now. You can't be doing hero stuff—"

"What? What are you talking about 'I can't be doing hero stuff?'" I said, leaning back from him, about to argue.

"What if you get hit? Meg, if you get hurt, what happens to the baby?"

I paused because I hadn't thought about it. I mean, it's not like I'd done this before. I didn't know how this shit worked. That's not what I meant. I know *how* it happened. Stop giving me that look.

His hands were on my face, that hitch in his breath he gets when he's truly, deeply scared about what could happen. "Meg, please, please, no hero stuff right now."

"Okay."

"Okay?" he asked, the relief in his voice so strong it practically resonated in the air.

"Okay."

He kissed me. I slid my hands up his shirt, and he chuckled. "Meg," he said, pulling back. "We're not done talking."

"I felt like we were."

"Brit and Sandra."

"What about them?"

"They're still planning our fake wedding."

Oh yeah, so when we got back from camping, Greg practically took Virgil hostage – okay, that's a lie, literally all Greg had to do was say "courthouse" and Virgil knew exactly what he meant and drove us straight there. Also, you know how usually you have to go get a license and things? Yeah, no, Fortress and Vengeance got to skip the line and any other waiting that would've been involved. Susan had unintentionally done us a solid by doing her absolute best to follow us around and catch cute couple moments along with all the monster fights to report for KBC. We're apparently the most popular and well-known pair in the city currently.

We basically got to get married in that exact minute, and once that was done, we had to decide who was telling Brit and Sandra.

I made Maniac do it.

Brit and Sandra had both sighed, said we're ridiculously

romantic – which, no, we're not – and then insisted on having a fake wedding. I already had a dress, and they had already managed to book a venue and caterer and were in the middle of talking to bakeries about a cake. They said to just view it as a super early vow renewal, and they both swore on their not-yet-dead mother's graves that they wouldn't breathe a word to Tony or Greg's mother.

But Brit totally blackmailed me and said that I had to let her parents' bridal shop use photos of Greg and me for ads in all their stuff as well as let the photographer be the one to provide a wedding photo to Susan, provided she would mention said bridal shop on air.

"Yeah, so?" I said, finally responding to Greg.

"Well, they're either going to need to push the date up, or we'll have to come clean to everyone."

"People have babies before the wedding all the time now."

"You're okay with that?" Greg asked me. "You're okay with the snide shit Tony's going to pull?"

"I don't care what he thinks about me."

"I care when he says it about you."

"So punch him."

Greg snorted. "I cannot punch him; I'll end up smashing his jaw. He'll have to eat through a straw for life."

"I'm not seeing the problem there," I said. "Besides, he's going to say shit anyway. Unless we can get Brit and Sandra to get everything moved up to, well, four weeks ago at least, the timing will be off, and I feel like Tony can do the math."

"What do we need to do?" Greg asked.

"Just tell them—" I started, but he interrupted me.

"No, not them. I'll handle them. What do we need to do for you and the baby? Doctor appointments? Do we just show up at the hospital in nine months?" He scrubbed at his face. "You have an IUD; that has to come out, right?"

"Yup, I have to call my doctor."

His brow was furrowed. "I'm not complaining about the results, but the chances – we've been careful."

"Camping trip," I said.

He looked at me, confused at first, and then his face cleared. "Oh. Oh, the beach."

I hadn't told Greg that Hera made an appearance and then left right before he found me standing by the lake that night. With the current situation, I wasn't entirely sure her blessing hadn't included a compulsion. The question was whether Greg had ended up included in it. At the time, I thought he had been reacting to the fact that he had woken up and I wasn't in the tent with him, because he had been acting normally overall. And there definitely hadn't been anything off about him during *that*.

Greg pulled his arm out from behind my back and heaved himself off the couch. "Come on, we might as well tell Virgil and get it over with before he tries to send us out for high-speed chases."

The last few weeks had been nice and quiet, actually. No monsters, no gods popping in, just the run of the mill bad guys. Convenience store robberies, muggings, a couple bike thefts. Even the villains seemed to have hunkered down, too busy planning their next world domination move to cause general mischief and mayhem.

Which probably meant something big was about to happen.

Look, no one ever accused me of looking at the glass as half full.

When we knocked on Virgil's door downstairs and he pulled it open, he seemed to have been expecting us.

"You have news, I take it," he said, stepping back from the door and motioning us in.

We went in and sat down on one of his couches, Greg laying his arm across my shoulders. Virgil had not gone for the studio look; his apartment was still divided into separate rooms, so we had to pass through an entryway into his living room. I suspect it's because he still has secret entrances to various places in the building, and I wouldn't be surprised if his entire apartment can be locked down into separate panic rooms if necessary.

The living room was home to just couches and chairs, plush rugs, and his tv and entertainment system. He set up a separate library and study combo in another room for all his books. He sat down on the couch across from us, leaning back against the cushions, one ankle resting on his knee, one hand resting on the arm of the couch.

"Well?" he said.

"Meg's pregnant," Greg said.

Virgil smiled, the corners of his eyes crinkling. "Congratulations. But I take it this is more than a social call to inform me?"

"She can't go out on calls."

Virgil steepled his fingers, the tips of his index fingers against his nose. "I don't know that I can accommodate that request—"

Next to me, Greg stiffened, his fingers flexing against my shoulder. "She cannot be running around chasing after villains in her condition."

Excuse me, condition? I didn't suddenly become incapable. I opened my mouth to shoot that retort straight at Greg. I was willing to work with him here on not going chasing after bad guys but not if he was going to treat me like I was suddenly helpless.

But Virgil had held his hands out, palms up, beseeching, "At this time. I don't know that I can accommodate it at this time. We have a few months before it will even be noticeable. Meg won't be centered as a target over that for a while yet."

"She's always a target," Greg said. "What happens if she gets hurt?"

Virgil had put a hand on his chin, considering. "I understand your concern. However, may I remind you, you cannot shove her into a cabinet?"

Greg shoved his hair back. "This is not the same—"

"Yes, it is," Virgil said. "Meg, are you going to stay here in your tower?"

I opened my mouth, shut it, and glared at Virgil because I knew what he was getting at. No matter what I promised Greg about staying safe, there was a very good chance I would break that promise in the heat of the moment.

Virgil wasn't done. "If you're the only one left here, and a call comes in while the rest of us are already occupied, are you just going to let it lie? Let innocent people die? Or are you going to rush off and do your job?" He had me stuck, because maybe, once upon a time, I would've said, "Not my circus, not my monkeys." But now? What else could I possibly do? Taking up this mantle still felt odd and stiff to me even though I knew I would go rushing right into the danger.

He had Greg trapped too.

"That's not," and Greg's voice cracked, "that's not fair to—"

Virgil leaned forward, "I am not saying I won't do my best. But your expectations that Meg can stop being what she is because you're becoming a family of three aren't fair."

Greg withdrew his arm from my shoulder, and leaned forward, elbows on his knees, hands clenched together. "Meg, I need to speak to Virgil alone," he said quietly.

"But—" I started.

"Please."

"You don't get to have a conversation about me and what I'm doing behind my back—"

"We will *not* be making any decisions for you," Virgil said. "But if you don't mind…" he motioned at the door.

"I'm not going anywhere when I'm the subject of the conversation," I said stubbornly.

Greg was still looking at his hands. "Please, Meg?" He turned his head, caught my eyes. "Please?" he repeated.

I glared at the two of them, but they didn't say anything else, and once the silence had stretched, I couldn't stand it anymore. "Fine," I snapped and stormed out of Virgil's apartment.

"We'll know if you're eavesdropping!" Virgil called after me before I slammed his front door shut.

CHAPTER TWO

When our apartment door finally opened, it wasn't Greg who came in. Virgil stayed back, watching me where I sat on the couch, from the doorframe. I stared back at him.

"May I come in?" he asked eventually.

"Yes," I said. "Where's Greg?"

Virgil stepped in, closing the door behind him. "I sent him on a peace offering run. I didn't want him in the building while I came to talk to you."

"About what?" I might have sneered it because I was still mad about being summarily dismissed from a conversation that was obviously going to be about me.

"He is worried about what this will mean when Poseidon comes calling for your debt."

"Oh," I said.

Virgil crossed his arms. "He intends to take it on."

I had suspected he might try to. "I won't let him."

"I know," Virgil said, crossing the room and sitting down on our coffee table so that he was seated across from me, the space narrow enough that our knees touched. "I didn't inform him of such. I am hoping that whatever this god is planning, his use for you will take long enough to come to fruition that Greg will not have to be disabused of this notion."

"That doesn't sound like you," I said. "Where's your

back up plan?"

"The two of you have thrown a monkey wrench into my back up plan."

I narrowed my eyes at him. "Why do you have a stash of pregnancy tests to start with if that's the case?"

Virgil eyed me steadily. "Meg, what kind of boy scout would I be if I didn't have those available?"

I snorted.

He sighed. "I do not advertise the extent of what I can do for a reason. People don't trust the person who knows what you're going to say before you say it. It's easy enough to brush it off in a small child as precociousness. Past a certain age, everything you reveal knowing is seen as holding malicious intent."

"You do blackmail a lot of people."

The corners of his eyes crinkled. "I will admit I unashamedly take advantage of the gifts I was given. Having said that, when were you going to tell me about Hera?"

I gaped at him, remembered to close my mouth, and thought about it. "Do you know everything I don't tell you?"

"It works best on things people are intentionally hiding," Virgil said. "Assume any white lie you've ever told me I've seen past."

Which was Virgil's roundabout-I'll-let-you-save-face way of saying yes.

"What about how convenient your timing always is?"

The corners of Virgil's lips lifted. "Oh that. That is just extremely good luck."

I didn't believe him. And from the amusement in his eyes, he knew I didn't.

"Back to the subject at hand before Greg comes home and realizes you've been hiding this from him. Explain what happened," Virgil said.

"Don't you already know?"

"Humor me."

"She gave me her blessing, on our last night of

17

camping."

Virgil sighed again. "How did you know she was there?"

"I woke up when her Guardian walked by the tent."

"Why did you go meet her on your own?"

I looked down at my feet. "It didn't seem like a bad idea at the time."

Virgil pinched the bridge of his nose. "Meg. What does it take to convince you it's a bad idea at the time?"

"Imminent death."

"I'm not sure that would stop you," he pointed out. "Did her blessing happen to involve any sort of compulsion?"

"I don't know," I said honestly.

Virgil nodded, one hand on his chin, elbow braced against his knee as he regarded me. "Will it afford you any protection from her husband?"

"It might," I said. "But I won't know unless…" I didn't want to say Zeus' name. I didn't want to somehow attract his attention with a call on the wind.

"Any protection from any of the others?"

"Unlikely," I said. "Poseidon's debt was first."

Virgil was thinking, his brow furrowed. "Well, one is better than none. Would Ares be willing to assist in ridding you of the debt?"

"I don't know that I won't just end up owing him instead."

"Hmm, the evil you know versus the one you don't." Virgil's lips had thinned. "The question is the cost. Would assistance deepen it?"

"I think we'd have to ask."

"And he might just do what Poseidon did and saddle you with a debt without giving you a chance to agree to the price first." The index finger of Virgil's other hand was tapping his leg. He stood up. "Greg is going to be sensitive when he gets home. Please try to be mindful of it. I don't need him pulling a you and running off to seek out any of them before we have a chance to discuss a team-based solution."

"You think he would go behind my back for this?"

"To keep the two of you safe? I think we've only scratched the surface of what Greg would be capable of if it meant you would be unharmed."

"He wouldn't—" I started to argue.

"Guilt will only restrain someone so far," Virgil said. "I, for one, do not want to test it. Grenadier did not get crushed against the wall because it was necessary."

∞

When Greg came back, he landed on the balcony and knocked on the door. I got it out of lockdown mode for him, and he came in.

I had promised I would lock that door any time he wasn't in the apartment with me, and so far, I've kept that promise. After Virgil's visit, it seemed even more imperative to remember it, to at least give him the illusion that I was safe.

Greg held an envelope out to me. "Here."

I took it, opened it, and pulled out what was inside: two tickets for *The Lion King* at the Lue Theatre in downtown. I stared at them; they were dated for four weeks from now.

He cleared his throat. "That was the earliest performance they had anything left for. And I don't know if the seats are any good. The lady at the box office said they were."

I smiled at him. "You're going to take me to a live musical?"

He gave me a tired smile back. "Yes."

I practically tackled him, wrapped my arms up around his back and hugged him. Gently, he wrapped his arms around me, his nose in my hair. "Careful or you'll crush your tickets."

I unwound my arms to check them, but they were fine. He plucked them from my fingers, reached over to set them down on the coffee table, then wrapped that arm back around me.

"Thank you," I said.

"For not letting you crush them?"

I snorted. "You know what I meant."

He chuckled, his arms tightening around me. He was silent for a moment. "I'm sorry," he said. "I just, I reacted without thinking about how what I was asking would affect you."

"I do keep pushing the limits of how many gray hairs I can give you."

He made a strangled noise. "That's just it, you're not doing it. It's—" His phone rang, interrupting whatever his thought had been. With a sigh, he pulled it out and looked at the screen, his brow furrowing as he swiped to answer. "Hello?"

The look on his face grew serious, "How many?" he asked. "When?"

I squirmed, leaning back against his arm. "What is it?"

He was busy listening to whoever was on the other end. "Yes, we can come now. Address?" Another moment and he had hung up, and slipped the phone back in his pocket.

"What is it?" I repeated.

"That was Mason. He's got a weird case and wants us to come look at it."

"Mason called us? And weird how?"

"He didn't say, just that there's only one victim," Greg said. "Come on, we need to tell Virgil we're going to see what he wants."

"Oh, you're taking me with you?" I teased.

"You want to stay in the tower?"

"You know, between you and Virgil repeating that, our headquarters has a name now."

"The Tower?"

"Yup."

Greg's phone pinged, and he pulled it back out. "Virgil says to go ahead and go." Then he looked at me suspiciously. "You're not asking how he knew."

"I'm not?" I said innocently.

"Did he tell you where the bugs are?"

"Nope." Because it was the truth, he wouldn't hear what was behind it.

"Hmm," he said, still eyeing me. "You know something I don't know."

"We're keeping Mason waiting."

"Suit up," he said, loosening his arms from around me.

I sighed and headed to our closet to pull out that ridiculous thing, got changed, pulled my jeans and long sleeve shirt back over it, and got my shoes back on. Greg scooped me up.

"Hey!"

He ignored my protest, carrying me to and then pulling open the door to the balcony and stepping out. "Ready?"

"Do I have a choice?"

"With me? Always."

"Hmm," I said. He kissed me and then leapt into the air.

∞

The address Mason had given Greg was for a brownstone building. He met us on the steps for the front door, leaning on the tall brick railing that edged them. He was in his typical suit pants, tie, and button-down shirt, this time wearing the jacket that matched the pants. His thinning brown hair was mussed, his suit wrinkled, like he had been dragged off a couch from a nap. The buttons were just on this side of starting to strain on his overweight frame; he probably needed to go up a size. The CSI and coroner vans were at the curb, a news van parked up the street, trying surreptitiously to collect footage of the current action.

"Thought you weren't the attention type," he grunted by way of greeting when Greg had landed and set me down.

"I keep trying to scare her off," I said, because I knew he was talking about Susan.

"She's like a tick. The harder you pull, the harder she clings."

"You said you had an unusual case?" Greg asked.

"Yeah, this way," Mason said, leading the way in and lifting the yellow cordon tape so Greg and I could slip under it. Well, he let *me* slip under it, he released it just enough that it caught Greg's face. "Oops," he said.

Greg ignored it, ducking farther under the tape and then waiting for Mason to come under and precede us.

Mason did, trotting up the wood stairs just off the entry, ignoring the officers and crime scene techs milling in the hall. "Neighbor called it in. Said they heard suspicious noises. The yahoo who took the first call treated it as a noise complaint." He was turning onto the landing of the second floor, following the banister around down the hallway back toward the front of the house, where an open door stood with a couple officers by it. Mason went in.

"Fortunately, our friendly neighborhood busybody called it back in, and this time had the sense to express deep, deep concern over the *screaming* they heard," he was saying, as I came into the room and saw what was waiting for us.

I came to a stop just a step into the room because when I saw what was left on the bed, I had started to back up but bumped into Greg, who placed his hands on my waist, then carefully slid around me.

It was most of a skeleton, the bones scattered over the comforter, which was so soaked with blood there was no way to tell what color it had started as. There were little pieces of flesh and gristle still clinging to the bones. If someone had described the scene to me, I would've thought they were talking about the carcass of a prey animal, but the skull left on one of the pillows was most definitely human, and it had been set up intentionally to face the door, grinning at whoever walked in.

The rest of the room was strangely clean. No blood on the single nightstand to the right of the bed. No cast-off, droplets or spattering on the floor, walls or ceiling. It was as if any other evidence had been washed away and only the bed and the remains were left to bear witness.

"Coroner agreed to wait until after you could come take a look before he packed everything up. He says it looks like something gnawed on the bones, but he can't confirm it until he's got everything at the morgue for the medical examiner," Mason said. "Which is why I called you, my esteemed friends."

Greg's lips twitched. "Esteemed?" he asked.

"Friends?" I asked.

"If this is some sort of monster shit again, this case gets handed over to White and her task force," Mason said. "So, your *professional*," he sneered the word, "opinions are required."

"Which opinion are you hoping for?" Greg asked.

"The one that ends in a dead monster," Mason said, "human or otherwise."

Greg grunted and stepped over to the bed, examining the remains. "Did the coroner say anything about what kind of gnaw marks these are?"

"Too big to be rats."

Greg held a hand to me. "Vengeance, come take a look, please."

I stepped forward, coming to stand beside him, even though I would've preferred to leave the room, and looked down at the skeleton. The bone closest to me looked like it was the thigh bone, but I'm basing it off the length and not any actual knowledge of human anatomy. I was trying to keep my face averted from the ribcage, which was situated in one large piece around the middle of the bed.

You would think I wouldn't be so squeamish after all I've done.

"They notice anything?" Greg asked me quietly, his voice a whisper in my ear.

I closed my eyes. An assurance that we could handle it was all they gave me, a taste of familiarity with whatever had done this. But it was enough: "Monster," I told him.

Mason was watching the two of us. "There's been some

noise about declaring monster attacks a type of domestic terrorism. That'll put a real cramp in your style once they start bringing in the alphabet agencies."

"White will get taken off the task force if that happens," Greg said.

"I think she's looking forward to that. Monster hunts aren't her style."

"They your style?" Greg asked.

Mason snorted. "No. Seeing what man does to his fellow man is bad enough for me. You need help with this one, don't call me." He held out a business card. "Here's the number for the medical examiner taking this on. Speak directly to him. I'm washing my hands of this one."

Greg took the card. "Didn't take you for the type to give up a case."

"And if you had brought anyone but her, I might have been the type not to." He looked us both over again. "I know when I'm in over my head. I'm no use to the people looking for answers if I get eaten by whatever the fuck it is this time."

I'm not entirely sure when I became the type of person people liked.

But all Greg said in response was, "Noted." He put his hand on the small of my back, steering me back out the door and down the stairs, lifting the tape so we could leave through the front door. The cameraman for the news truck had managed to sneak his way up the sidewalk for a closer view, and he trained his camera on us as we were exiting. Greg sighed, "It's KBC again." But he pulled me against him, so I was pressed to his chest and took off.

∞

When we landed back at the Tower, we went through our apartment and straight down the stairs to Virgil's floor. He was at his door, leaning against the frame, arms crossed as he waited for us.

"Meg says we have monsters," Greg told him.

"Do you know what kind?"

"No," I said. "Just that it is one, and the feeling they gave me was that it would be—easy—to take out?

"It ate a person," Greg said.

"What were the remains like?" Virgil asked.

"Animal kill. Scraped clean as much as possible. Mason said the coroner told him the bones had been gnawed on."

"Meg, how many tales do you remember where the monster ate people?"

"A lot."

"Such as?"

"The Minotaur, Scylla, Cyclops the Sphinx, Empusa, Lamia – am I supposed to keep going?"

"No. I think I get the point. Would any of those be unlikely based on the location?"

"Scylla is a sea monster."

Virgil waited, staring at me. I stared back, not because I didn't want to answer him but because I was trying to think it through.

I had tried really hard to forget any of the information about Greek mythology I had in my head. I went as scorched earth with my parents as I could, to the point where I had legally changed my last name, but not my first. At the time, I wasn't sure why I felt the need to hold onto it. Now I suspected it had to do with the Furies not wanting to let go of it, but the whispers had stayed silent on that subject.

And no, I didn't take Greg's last name once we were married. Changing it once before was difficult enough.

"Cyclops wouldn't fit inside; they're supposed to be giants," I finally said.

"I'm not sure we can discount them," Virgil said. "Based on the fact that we know some of the information in the tales is wrong."

"The Sphinx usually guards a road. At least, she did in the tale."

"And the Minotaur is supposed to be imprisoned in a labyrinth," Virgil said, "but we know none of the information we have tells the whole truth since the Gorgon could create Hydras."

I made a frustrated noise. "Then we can't discount any of them."

Virgil had pulled out his phone and was texting. "Ranger and Maniac need to be in on this."

"If our team keeps growing, you're going to need a conference room," Greg said.

"If my team gets large enough to need a conference room, I'm going to be at the point where we would need additional funding. Financially, I can't support more than a five-person team."

"You're going to need at least two more people to cover what Meg and I do; the expense is coming, either way," Greg pointed out. "We could apply for a grant."

Virgil had a hand up at his chin. "We would need to be selective about which heroes we approach. And unlike my collection of retainer fees, we would have to provide data to back up renewing the grant each year."

"We could start providing private security."

"That would require travel from our team members and sending them out in singles rather than doubles." Virgil was thinking again. "It would be doable, but there'd be the potential of stepping on toes in the larger cities."

"I think the other heroes would get over it."

"Some of you are territorial," Ranger said from behind us. He and Maniac had come up the stairs from the apartments below.

Oh, yeah, Virgil put Ranger on an entirely different floor from Greg and me even though there were three other available apartments up on the top floor with us. He had claimed within earshot of me that it was so we could have privacy as newlyweds, but considering I knew for a fact he had offered one of them to Maniac, that was a lie. Whatever read he was getting off Ranger or Greg meant he felt it would be better to keep Ranger separated from the two of us.

Virgil can't put anyone else on his floor because of the lab, security, his apartment and the whole apartment set aside for clients who need a long-term stay. Otherwise, he might have put Ranger where he could keep a direct eye on him.

"Like who?" Greg asked. "I've never had a problem."

"Edgewave over in Garro. He's got a problem with other heroes coming into his town," Ranger said, crossing his arms over his chest, his dark eyes focused on Greg. Clothed only in a black t-shirt and biker pants, he wasn't wearing his reinforced leather jacket. He must have left it behind in his apartment, his black hair mussed, stubble on his jaw.

"Other heroes or just you?" Greg asked.

Ranger smirked. "You know, until I got here, I never rubbed anyone the wrong way."

"They probably just didn't tell you because they knew you'd be leaving soon."

"I can always leave if my skills aren't wanted."

"No," Virgil said. "You and your skills are valued. The posturing needs to stop. There are enough issues at hand without dissension in the ranks," he pointed a finger at Ranger, "and you had lost before you even started the game, so get over it."

Ranger's eyes were shadowed, but all he did was jerk his head at Virgil.

Maniac had her arms crossed, her weight shifted toward one leg. Her cherry red coils had gotten a recent color infusion so that they glowed bright against her brown skin. "Did I miss a memo?"

I hate red, but on Maniac it looks really good. I've gotten over flinching any time she pops around a corner unexpectedly. Maybe because the shade of her hair is so different from the color of Red Eye's eyes.

Fuck him, he's dead, I won.

"This meeting is the memo," Virgil said. "We have a

new monster on the loose eating people."

"Just the one that we're aware of," Greg said.

"There will be more," Virgil pointed out, and Greg just grunted.

"Are we at least done with the snakes?" Ranger asked.

"Yes. Whatever this is, it had teeth," Greg said.

"Snakes have teeth," Ranger said.

"You know—" Greg started, and I could hear the heat in his voice.

"The type of teeth this monster has left gnaw marks on the remains from what I've been told," Virgil interrupted smoothly, "so another snake-based monster seems unlikely. Greg, did Mason say when he would have an update for you?"

"He said he's washing his hands of this one. It's probably getting handed to White."

"She was robbery."

"They started a villain-created monsters task force after Rat King."

Virgil pinched the bridge of his nose. "Could you please remember to inform me of these kinds of events?"

"We got distracted when the snake came back to life," I said.

"And conveniently forgot," Virgil said pointedly.

"At least it wasn't intentional?"

"We're getting off track," Greg said. "Mason said the coroner will give me a call when he's got results. Although if White is taking over, she might be the one we're talking to."

"Call her," Virgil said. "Make sure we're kept in the loop. Did Mason tell you anything that would help us keep an eye out for another occurrence?"

"Neighbor called it in, said they heard screaming."

"I'll make sure to monitor the 911 and dispatch feeds in that case."

My stomach chose that moment to roll over, and I had to do that hard swallow thing you do when you're trying not to vomit. Greg turned to me, one hand on my back, bent so his face was level with mine.

"Bucket?" he asked.

I shook my head. "No," I said through clenched teeth, my stomach still roiling. "I just need a minute."

I had everyone's attention now, though.

"You sick, Meg?" Ranger asked.

I shook my head again. The feeling was slowly passing.

"Ginger might help with that," Virgil said.

"Ginger would help with what?" Ranger asked. Maniac kicked his shin. "Ow! What was that for?" he demanded.

"Don't be an ass," she said. "Give her a second."

"Give her a second for what?" Ranger said, still confused. Apparently, he was the only one out of the loop.

"Did Virgil tell you?" I asked Maniac, trying to concentrate on that rather than the new surge from my stomach.

She snorted. "No, I got enough aunts and cousins that I know that look."

"Should she go lie down?" Greg asked her over my head.

"Lie down for *what?*" Ranger demanded, having finally come to the realization that he was the only one unaware of what was going on.

"Meg's pregnant," Greg said, ripping off the band-aid.

I was too busy looking at the floor to see whatever expression Ranger's face was making.

"Which brings us to the next item on the agenda," Virgil said, sailing past Ranger's stunned silence. "Eventually Meg will have to take leave from hero work to reduce the risk to herself and the baby."

I don't think Virgil had that set up for the agenda for today yet.

"Who're you going to make tell the in laws?" Maniac asked. "Because I was already up for that duty."

"I'm handling that," Greg said. "Since now they'll have to know we got married without inviting them."

"Technically, they don't have to," I said, finally

straightening up. "We can just let them think we've been living in sin."

Greg snorted.

"Are you sure you even like your family?" Ranger asked. "Telling us first and all."

Greg was silent for a long moment; then he slid his arm around my back so his hand rested on my waist. "You're family."

Both Maniac and Ranger had separate types of surprise on their face, and I'm pretty sure I looked just as surprised as they did because from what I knew about Maniac's past and the constant jostling between Ranger and Greg, I figured the only one on this team he liked other than me was Virgil.

"I didn't think you even liked me," Ranger said.

"You're tolerable," Greg said.

Ranger grinned at him. "Just tolerable?" It was the first time I had seen him give Greg a genuine smile.

Greg glossed by it. "You've stood with us for the important things. It makes you family."

"So, misfits are your type."

Greg's lips twitched. "Hanging out with people on the straight and narrow just keeps not working out for me."

"You should work on that," Ranger told him.

"I don't know, I'm kind of happy with where I landed."

"As heartwarming as it is that the two of you are finally on a similar wavelength," Virgil said. "We do have a couple of matters at hand. Meg and Greg will be taking time for doctor appointments, so you and Maniac will need to be available to cover the shifting schedule."

"No problem," Ranger said.

"Brit and Sandra are gonna be pissed," Maniac told me.

CHAPTER THREE

When I called my doctor and told them I was pregnant and needed to get my IUD out, they got me in surprisingly quickly, with an appointment for the next day.

Greg flew us there, landing in the parking lot. My OB/GYN's office is in one of those multiple medical office parks, where you have several different doctors and health systems bumping up against each other in some sort of strip mall-like setting. On either side of my doctor was a urologist and then a dentist. A couple doors down there's a chiropractor. His business is always hopping, so I've long suspected he's doing more than cracking bones.

I made Greg sit in the waiting room when they took me back. Look, no one but the doctor, nurse and I needed to be present for IUD removal.

Of course, they made me pee in a cup before they took me to the exam room, but it's not like they were going to be telling me something I didn't already know.

"So, Megaera," Dr. Hawk said as she came in the room, flipping through my chart. "You're pregnant, and according to these dates, you should be just over ten weeks along."

"Yup," I said. I mean, what she was saying tied in with that night on the beach.

She sat down on the stool, rolling her way over to me.

She's one of those calming-type people: gentle eyes, serene voice, movements always steady, somehow ageless skin even though she's got gray hair. She set my chart down and regarded me. "How do you feel about that?"

Like I don't need a therapist is what I thought, but I didn't say it to her. "Fine," I said.

"My receptionist said a man came in with you for your appointment today."

"Yup, that's my husband." I couldn't help it; I felt the grin spread across my face when I said the word.

She noticed and smiled back at me. "So, would you say this is a happy occasion?"

I briefly considered asking if I told her yes if it would stop the questions so we could get the whole appointment over with but didn't say those words either. "Yup," I said instead.

"Hmm," she said. "If it's not, there are options."

"Nope, don't need those. I don't need the domestic violence spiel either. I'm good."

She looked startled for a moment, and then her calm mask was back in place. "Okay, if you're certain. I'm just going to do a quick pelvic exam and get your IUD out, and we'll move on from there."

We're gonna skip right past those details to the next thing she said to me.

"I can't locate the IUD's strings. We're going to have to perform an ultrasound."

"What?" I asked anxiously.

"There's nothing to worry about," she said reassuringly. "Sometimes they get expelled, and that's what we'll be checking for. And since we'll be using the equipment anyway, we can check on the fetus. Would you like me to have the nurse bring your husband back?"

"Yes."

They at least didn't make me cool my heels waiting for Greg to get back there for too long. The nurse opened the door for him, and he came in looking confused and worried.

"They said I needed to come back here?"

"They can't find the IUD."

His face cleared. "Didn't know you could lose them."

"Apparently." I had my suspicions that mine had help getting lost in the first place. The timing was too convenient to have been a coincidence.

He snagged the stool with a foot, rolling it back over by the exam table so that he was seated between me and the door. "So, what are they doing?"

"Ultrasound. You know the nurse isn't going to come in here waving a scalpel, right?"

He chuckled but stayed where he was.

At the sound of a cart being wheeled down the hallway, I tensed. Greg was on his feet, pulling me against his chest. I swallowed, focusing on the sound of his heart under my ear. "I've got you," he murmured into my hair.

There was a knock on the door, and then they swung it open without waiting for an answer. The ultrasound tech was a cheerful-looking woman, all smiles, her coloring matching her rosy attitude. "Helllooo," she called, wheeling the cart in. It looked so completely different from the one Red Eye had that my muscles almost immediately relaxed. This one was all beige plastic, a computer on top and little holders for the wand and a bottle of gel. Nothing like the rusted metal that would make its way into my nightmares on occasion.

Greg had released part of his hold on me, stepping to one side, although he kept an arm wrapped around my back.

"I need to go where you're standing, honey," she said.

He looked flustered, and it took him a minute to make a decision about where he was going. He ended up behind the exam table, standing at my back.

"First timer, huh?" she said, still smiling, settling the cart next to the table, pulling out a folded blue paper sheet and handing it to me. It resembled that bib the dentist puts on your chest when you go get your teeth cleaned except bigger. "Just lie back, scooch your pants down a bit and tuck that in so the gel doesn't get on your clothes."

I didn't mention I've had worse substances get on my clothes. Of course, some of those clothes ended up – you know what? You know exactly what happened to those clothes; let's not get into this again. Oh yeah, they had me go ahead and get dressed when they couldn't find the IUD; I haven't been sitting around in a hospital gown this whole time.

Ultrasound gel is cold, by the way.

Greg made a noise when she pressed the wand down.

"Oh relax," she said. "I'd have to be shoving this in a whole lot harder to cause any sort of issue. Babies are well protected." She was moving the wand around, leaning the top back and forth as she examined the screen, clicking and typing. She clucked her tongue. "Yup, definitely don't see an IUD," she muttered. I don't know if she had meant to say that out loud. Then she gave the cart a turn so we could see and pointed at the screen. "There's your baby. There's the head here, and the butt is here."

We both stared at it, Greg's fingers flexing against mine softly, not the way they usually did when he was angry about something.

"And this," she clicked something else, and the sound filled the room, rhythmic and quick, so different from the solid boom of Greg's when I would press my ear to his chest, "is the heartbeat."

There was dawning realization on Greg's face, and then his brow furrowed, concentrating.

"So, technically I'm not supposed to say anything, but it looks good. Nice and healthy." She smiled at us again as she withdrew the wand and the sound stopped. Greg's head was cocked to the side, that look of concentration still on his face.

"And these," she said, pulling a strip of black and white images from a little printer on the middle shelf of the cart, "are your first pictures of baby." Greg reached over me to take them.

"Here," she said, handing me tissues and helping me get

all the gel wiped off. Then she was packing up, standing and pushing the cart back out of the room, closing the door behind her before I was even done getting my pants back up and buttoned.

"Your heartbeat is so much louder," Greg said, and then he had pressed his ear to my stomach, his chin in my lap. He laughed. "I can hear it. I can hear both of them, they—your hearts beating together—they're musical."

For the first time, I was jealous of his ability to hear what others couldn't. He pulled his head off my stomach and looked me in the eye, one hand on my face. "Meg," he said. There was an understanding in his voice that made me have to blink away tears. He wrapped his arms around me, hugging me to him.

"They're going to want the exam room back," I said.

He chuckled. "Don't they have to tell you you're allowed to check out?"

"Like that would stop me if I didn't want to stay."

He chuckled again, then sobered. "I think you'll want to consider a closer doctor. I don't know how far along you can be before I should stop flying you around."

"I like this doctor," I said. "Just don't fly any faster than a car."

There was a knock on the door, and Dr. Hawk was sliding back in, looking at a chart. "So, looks like your IUD did pull a disappearing act. Fetus looks great, estimated due date is April 27th." She handed me a slip of paper. "You're free to go; just let the receptionist know so she can schedule you for your next appointment in four weeks." She had left before I could hop off the exam table.

I towed Greg out of the room and down the hall back to the front desk. I got my check out paper handed in and a new appointment card with the next date written on it then led him out into the parking lot, where he pulled me back against him and scooped me up.

"You ready?" he asked.

"You're going to fly like a little old lady, aren't you?"

"Absolutely," he said and took off.

∞

Bacchus was in our apartment when we got back.

Greg and I had come in through the balcony door, with me preceding him, and he almost tripped over me when I came to a sudden stop barely through the door.

Bacchus had been sitting on the couch, and at my entrance had risen and set his bottle of whiskey down on our coffee table. When Greg realized why I had paused, he moved to set himself between the two of us. I could see the tremor up the muscles of his back. I set a hand on his shoulder, half leaning out from behind so I could see Bacchus. He was still in that 70s stoner outfit, bell bottom jeans, open vest with bare chest and stomach exposed, his black hair mussed and his green eyes sly.

He had pulled out his pack of cigarettes and was searching his pockets again. "Got a light?"

"No," I said. "You know I don't. Why are you here?"

"You left your gift," he said, and there was a swirl of something I couldn't place in his tone.

"Damn it," I said. "Our apartments got blown up. I didn't even realize it survived the blast."

The basket of wine and grapes had started in the hall, and Virgil had intended to store it in Ranger's apartment but had ended up moving it out into the lab because he had wanted to examine it first. It had still been in there when Grenadier had tried to take Maniac out. The bottle of whiskey Bacchus had left on the roof had been in there too.

Something about Bacchus relaxed, and he flung himself back down on our couch, putting his feet up on our coffee table.

"Get—" Greg started, but paused at the way I squeezed his shoulder.

Bacchus reached forward and snagged the tickets off the

table, holding them up to examine them.

"Put those down," I said.

Bacchus leaned his head back so he was looking at me upside down over the pillows of the couch. Under my hand, I could feel Greg trembling. Bacchus was letting his eyes rove between us. Then he moved, leaning forward to set the tickets back on the table, and popped back up on his feet. He turned so he was facing us and watched us curiously.

"That explains it," he said.

"What explains what?" I was trying to stay calm. Greg needed me to be calm, confident. I hadn't brought the whispers out yet, but if Bacchus was going to talk in riddles, I was going to punch him.

He waved vaguely in Greg's direction, who tensed more if that was even possible. Bacchus noticed, baring his teeth in a grin. "Relax, Guardian. I come in peace." He flicked his eyes back to me. "That is a preferred phrase amongst the mortals, correct?"

"What explains what?" I repeated.

"Always business," Bacchus said.

"Ares had the same complaint," I said.

His smile widened. "How rare, that Ares and I have something in common."

"Are we going to verbally fence all day? Because I have things to do."

"Projects to get to? Mortals to save?" He came around the couch, stepping toward us as he spoke. Greg's hand had moved to my hip, and he was trying to get me to back up, but I stood my ground, leaning further out and then stepping just past him, standing at his side, his arm across my front, hand still on my hip, to keep my eyes on Bacchus.

"Monsters to slay?" Bacchus continued.

"What do you know about them?" I asked.

Bacchus shrugged. "Abominations. Feasting on the flesh of mortals, they breed in the dark like, what is it the mortals say? Rabbits?"

"I believe that's the colloquial. What are they?"

"An infestation. You'll want to take them out quickly, before their numbers are overwhelming."

I made an irritated noise in my throat. "Do they have a name?"

"No one, for they are many."

I glared at him because that didn't answer my question.

Bacchus rolled his eyes. "The clue is in the phrase. If I tell you directly, then we have to bargain, and I hate holding onto those things. Debts are trite."

"Poseidon didn't tell me directly," I said.

"Yes, he did," Bacchus said. "He told you exactly where the Gorgon was located. Hardly his fault you're out of practice. Or did you ever practice from the beginning? From what I recall, you were never much of a bargainer either."

"Why are you—helping?"

There was a flash of mischief in his eyes. "I'm hard up for entertainment."

"Well, find a different show," I said.

His lips twitched, the corners lifting as he bared his teeth again. "I like this one."

"I don't get your interest in it."

Bacchus had come up to us, and Greg was trying to herd me backwards, the nudge of his fingers on my hip gentle but persistent. I think he was afraid to try to move me, no matter what the ultrasound tech had said about babies being well protected. He gave up on trying to convince me to move and stepped directly in front of me so that I was staring at his back.

Bacchus had to look up to lock eyes with him. His grin widened. "Guardian."

"Fortress," Greg said through gritted teeth.

"Fortress is a name; Guardian is a title."

"I'm not interested in your titles."

"You should be," Bacchus said, and he vanished.

Greg was still for a moment, both of us waiting to see if Bacchus would come back, and when nothing happened, Greg sat down on the floor.

"God damn it," he said.

I knelt next to him, one hand on his shoulder. "At least we don't owe him anything?"

Greg snorted. "That is not helping." He scrubbed at his face. "If he found where we are, again, can the rest of them?"

"Yes," I said honestly.

"I can't—" Greg took a breath, wrapped his arm around me and pulled me to him so that I was nestled against his side. "I know you said if we left, they would find you anyway. I didn't realize they would just show up in our home."

"We left the balcony door unlocked," I said.

He was silent, I think debating whether locking down the door and exiting through the rooftop door would keep gods out of our apartment or just hinder our escape route when they showed up. "Meg, will the baby be safe from them?"

"Yes," I said fiercely because I would make sure of it.

The truth of that must have been what he heard and not the intention behind it. Or he chose not to, choosing instead to hold to the belief, the illusion, that the gods would have no interest in our child. He sighed and nodded, turning his face to plant a kiss on the top of my head. Then he moved, shifting so he could reach into his pocket, and pulled out the ultrasound photos he had so carefully folded and put away. They had gotten wrinkled from when he had practically collapsed on the floor.

He cleared his throat. "Where can we put these? I know Tony and Peter had theirs up on the fridge for their kids, but if we have gods popping in and out, I don't want them to know if they don't already."

"Virgil's fridge?" I asked. "The baby's going to end up calling him Grandpa anyway."

Greg snorted, "Papa Virgil?" His shoulders started shaking, his ribs vibrating against me as he laughed. I smiled at him, giggling.

"Exactly. He can teach him all about timing. And how

to drive."

"Virgil is not teaching him how to drive," Greg said, then paused, looking back down at me. "You said he."

I shrugged. "It's easier than saying the baby all the time." And I had a feeling, but I didn't want to say anything. It would be putting too much stock in motherly instincts for me, at least at that point in time.

"Hmm," he said, pulling his arm off me and heaving himself off the floor before offering me a hand up. My knee chose that moment to pop, and his eyes darkened, lips thinning.

"You can't keep blaming yourself," I told him.

"If I had told you the truth sooner, he wouldn't have gotten a hold of you to begin with."

"You don't know that," I told him, but what he said gave me pause. How many things was I hiding from him now? And what could happen if I didn't tell him the truth of it? My intentions were for his peace of mind, but we all know where good intentions lead.

"Meg," he said, and he sounded frustrated and tired. "Would you have left the compound like you did if I hadn't hidden what Red Eye was doing from you?"

"Maybe not like that, but I may have done something stupid anyway."

He scrubbed his face, pushing his hair back. "What about now? Will you at least consider that you're not the only one at risk right now?" He was searching my face, and I could see the worry, the fear in his eyes.

"Yes," I said.

"Will you let me stand between you and the gods?"

"Yes." It was the answer he needed, even if the gods had other ideas. I didn't realize what I had just promised him until the word was out of my mouth, and I saw the satisfaction in his eyes.

Damn it.

He wasn't going to give me a chance to back track either, because he was tugging me toward the door. "Come on, we need to tell Virgil we had an unwelcome visitor."

There was a knock at the door, and Greg paused, looking back at me.

"What?" I said.

"How is he doing it?"

"He said it's just good timing," I said, dodging the real question.

Greg narrowed his eyes at me.

"Am I allowed in?" Virgil's voice was muffled by the door. "Or do I need to wait for Gregor to get over his suspicions?"

"Like we could keep you out," I called.

The lock clicked back, and Virgil opened the door and stepped in, leaving the door gaping behind him. "I have news from the coroner."

"That was fast," Greg said.

"Perks of having the lead detective of the task force on your side."

"How many favors did she have to pull to jump to the head of the line?"

"Just one," Virgil said.

"Six degrees of Kevin Bacon?" I asked.

Greg gave me a confused look. "Six degrees of what?"

"You're both too young to even remember that," Virgil said.

"It's still around," I said.

"I'm still not seeing what this has to do with White and the coroner," Greg pointed out.

"White asked Virgil for the favor," I said. "He's why the coroner jumped her case up. Therefore, six degrees of Kevin Bacon, or separation."

"Still don't see the connection there," Greg said.

"It's not funny if I have to explain it."

"I – you know what, never mind. I do want to know what you have on the coroner."

"No, you don't," Virgil said. "The coroner tells me that

the teeth marks are human-like."

"But they're not human?" Greg asked.

"No. He said they're too broad and somewhat shovel-like. They don't match anything they've got on file."

"That doesn't help us narrow anything down," I said.

"It does not," Virgil said agreeably; then he stood there, waiting and smiling genially at us. When neither of us said anything, he sighed. "I believe you had news for me as well?"

"That asshole god was here," Greg said.

"I think we can refer to him by name at this point," I said. "Since it appears he's just going to show up regardless of whether we've called him."

"What did he want?" Virgil asked.

"To give us a clue, apparently," I said.

"Which is?"

"They're no one, for they are many."

"Did he happen to say anything more useful?"

"He called them abominations, an infestation and said we would need to take them out quickly before they were overwhelming," Greg said.

"Cheerful," Virgil said. "Anything that might help locate this infestation?"

"They breed in the dark."

Virgil sighed again. "If we're dealing with sewers and subways again, I'll need to speak with the Mayor about getting some of those tunnels sealed up. The maze down there is—" his hand went up to his chin – "maze," he repeated. He looked at me. "An abomination...Minotaur?"

"Bacchus said an infestation. There's only ever been a single one in the tales," I said.

"How many Hydras did we kill?"

"Three."

"How many were there in the legends?"

"One."

"How many do you think we would've fought if we hadn't killed the Gorgon when we did?"

I opened my mouth, then closed it. "I don't know."

"Let's operate on the assumption that we're dealing with at least one Minotaur, and it's down in the subway or sewers. I'm going to make sure we have current blueprints for both. What do you remember about the tale?"

"It was in the center."

"That should make locating it easy. How often does it need to eat?"

"Depending on the version being told, fourteen people every year or every nine years."

"So, urgency will be required before thirteen more people die." He started for the door, paused and turned back toward us. "I believe there was something else?"

Greg held out the photos. "Will you keep these safe for us?"

Virgil took them, then looked down and examined them for a moment.

"Greg said you can hang them on your fridge," I said.

I saw Virgil's lips twitch, the corners of his eyes crinkling. "A place of honor, certainly." He stowed them carefully in the pocket of his duster jacket. "For now, I'll be examining maps of the various systems to find the center, along with the best route in and out. Once I've determined that, we'll set up for our excursions."

"Don't forget Maniac's snacks," I said.

CHAPTER FOUR

Virgil called us all down to security once he had gotten set up. The security room has a much larger set up than it used to. He has cameras monitoring the entire building, interior and exterior, both for all the office floors below us and in the hallways for our floors. As far as I'm aware, he did not set up cameras in our apartments themselves.

With gods randomly popping in, I'm not sure which route I would've rather he take.

In addition to the monitors, he's got a large blank wall set up for hanging maps and blueprints.

And apparently, an armory?

I took a moment to stare at it. It looked like a mix between a military gun locker and a medieval weapon cache, set up with rifles, shotguns, pistols, swords, maces, and even some spears.

"What is that?" Greg said.

"Preparation," Virgil said.

"With guns?"

"The ammo is stored separately."

"Do you even know how to use those?"

"Yes."

Whatever Greg was going to protest with next was interrupted by Ranger and Maniac's entrance.

"What's the plan, Stan?" Ranger asked.

"The plan," Virgil said, tapping the blueprints on the wall, "is to check the exact center of each of these systems for a Minotaur."

"A what?" Maniac asked.

"It's part bull—" Virgil started.

Maniac waved him off. "I know what it is. I took history, too. It's more that now we've got one of those to worry about?"

"It is the assumption that we're operating under at this time." Virgil turned back to the maps. "Now, we will need to check here," he put a pin into the center of the active subway system, "here," another pin went up, this time into the unused section, "here," a pin into the storm water sewer system, "and I would say we need to check the center of the sewage system, but the way that's set up, nothing can live in there. It would drown."

"Thank God for that at least," Ranger muttered.

Greg was looking at the locations Virgil had marked. "You don't think he'll be over near where the Rat King was nesting?"

"That entrance is the center of the city, not the center of the systems themselves, but we can add it to the list." Virgil added another pin.

"Are we all going?" Maniac asked.

"Yes, in teams. I want to check all the locations simultaneously. Ranger and Meg, you've got the storm water system. Greg, you're in the active subway. Maniac and I are taking the old subway system." He turned to Maniac. "You topped off?"

"Yup," she said. "Big lunch."

Oh yeah, Maniac's power tends to burn through a lot of energy. Literally.

Look, these are the puns. If you don't like them, you can leave.

In general, if she's going to be using it, she literally does

45

have to pack snacks, so Virgil's been making sure to keep us well-stocked in easy-to-transport foods like protein bars. She says even straight up candy works because the sugar gets converted to energy quickly.

Both Greg and Virgil are having to compromise their no sugar rules all over the place.

She tends to keep up with meals because otherwise her power starts burning through her reserves, and in a couple days, she starts losing weight. If she were to go a week without food, she would start getting the skeletal, long-term starvation victim look because it would start going after her muscle.

Her power was a rough one to grow up with, too.

She told me about the time she accidentally burnt down her cousin's treehouse. She laughs about it now, but I get the feeling no one found it very funny at the time, and there's a shade to her laugh that makes me think it's still not funny. But I'm not going to tell her how to view it.

Virgil started handing out printed and traced maps of the paths we needed to take. "Here. Follow these exactly so you don't get lost."

"String," I said.

"I do not have rolls of string that would be long enough for this," Virgil said. "I wasn't expecting a Labyrinth."

"Thought you were prepared for anything," I said.

"I admit, sometimes I fall down on the job," Virgil said, the corners of his eyes crinkling.

"All we would need to do is find a manhole nearby anyway," Ranger said looking the map over.

"There aren't any," Virgil said, "but you will be going into one of the larger reservoirs."

"Meg can't swim," Greg and Ranger said at the same time.

"If you have to go into the water down there, we have an entirely different problem," Virgil pointed out. "Meg, I feel it may be valuable that we set aside time for swim lessons."

I grumbled because I had been purposely avoiding that.

I knew I needed to do it, but any time I had been getting near a body of water lately, my heart and breath would speed up, and I kept having to stop and practice breathing to calm down.

Thanks, Poseidon, because I needed more things to have panic attacks over.

It hadn't bothered me at the lake during camping, so the only thing I could think was we had been far enough inland that the whispers and I didn't associate it with the sea.

"Fine," I said eventually because everyone seemed to be waiting for me to answer.

"Is everyone ready?" Virgil asked. "Okay, then down to the Hummer. Meg, Ranger we will be—"

"Nope," Ranger said. "Meg and I can take the bike; we're not going into the sewers and then waiting for a pickup after."

"I expect you to notify me when you go in and when you're done," Virgil said.

Greg made a noise. "I don't know that the bike—"

"I'll ride slow," Ranger said. "I'll even stop at red lights. But do you really want us cooling our heels in this weather while we wait for the rest of you to get done? What if Meg catches cold?"

Okay, so the temperature had cooled a bit because we're mid-September, but come on, it's not that cold out. We're not going to freeze to death if it takes them a bit to come get us.

But Ranger had Greg's number, at least when it comes to me. Greg scrubbed at his face. "No, I don't want that. Jacket," he said.

"What?" I said, confused by the subject change.

"Go get a jacket," Greg told me.

"I'm wearing sleeves," I argued.

"Jacket," Ranger said, arms crossed and apparently taking Greg's side.

"I am *not* wearing my only good jacket into the sewers," I said.

Ranger muttered, "Jesus, Meg. Wait here." He stomped

out of the security room and down the hall. I heard the door for the stairwell open and slam shut. He was back up a few minutes later, a black, leather jacket in hand. He held it out to me.

"What is this?" I asked as I took it. It felt much heavier than it should be.

"A jacket. It's reinforced, so if you wreck, you'll slide instead of getting splattered. It was supposed to be a gift for attack dog."

I examined it. "I don't think this is going to fit Greg."

Ranger made a frustrated noise. When we all watched him, he got snappish. "You're going to make me explain it? It was for Greg so he could give it to you. I know how he feels about the bike, and I thought this might make him feel better about it."

"Thought you would just reverse us," I said.

"I would," Ranger said. "That doesn't mean it wouldn't make the rest of us less concerned about it happening in the first place."

I opened my mouth to say something back, I'm not sure what, just that I felt the need to argue, but Greg laid a hand on my shoulder. "Meg," he said, then quietly to Ranger, "Thank you."

"You're welcome," Ranger said. "Can we get going? Now that I have to find new Christmas presents?"

Greg plucked the jacket from my grasp and held it out so I could slip my arms into it. "Who plans this far ahead for Christmas?" I asked zipping the jacket up. "And how did you get my size?"

"Ranger asked me, and I asked Brit and Sandra," Maniac said, "and some of us don't do everything at the last possible second."

"You've already gone Christmas shopping?" I asked.

"You haven't?" Maniac asked.

"No." I mean, it's been years since I had to go Christmas shopping in the first place. The first Christmas Greg and I had spent together had been shortly after the whole Red Eye thing, so we had still been hunkered down in Virgil's bunker. No one had gone anywhere, and all three of us had kind of ignored the whole holiday.

Greg hadn't even gone home to see family that year. He was still having nightmares at the time, so maybe he was worried about what would happen if he had gone for a visit.

"You're going to want to get on that," Maniac said.

∞

Greg had headed up a floor to exit through our balcony after giving me a kiss and telling Ranger to keep me safe.

Maniac and Virgil ended up going in the Hummer. Yes, his order finally came in. Something about identifying details needing to be scrubbed out? I don't know. What I do know is it got a new paint job in, predictably, black. But it's still very, very noticeably military grade.

The four of us rode down in the private elevator for our floors, which is connected to a garage separated from the main garage for the offices. One condition Virgil had for Henry the real estate developer was that there be no way to get to our apartments from the offices themselves. Even our stairwell is a whole separate thing going down to street level.

Once we got down there, Virgil and Maniac had peeled off in the direction of the Hummer, and Ranger and I climbed on the bike. He gave me long enough to get seated and a tight grip before he took off, spinning the tires with how hard he gassed it. We went up the exit ramp, and the bike went airborne for a moment.

It's a good thing the streets are wide in this part of town because we went into oncoming traffic before he got it turned.

Ranger totally lied about stopping for red lights, by the way.

We were headed for the theatre and art district because that one had the closest manhole we could go down for the section we were headed into. Once we were there, Ranger had to find a place to park the bike. He ended up jumping the curb and going straight across the main plaza, which caused a lot of shouting from various pedestrians out there viewing the current exhibit.

He parked us next to a statue of a white bull with golden horns and hooves. A hulking thing, its head was lowered, feet pawing at the ground, tail flagged, it's body language one of ready-to-charge mode.

I had to shake my arms out once I let go of him; they were sore. He watched me, grinning. "You know, you don't have to do a death grip."

"Maybe if you didn't drive that way, I wouldn't," I said. "Besides, you said hold on tight."

"That's not tight, that's strangulation," he said, leading the way to the manhole cover a few feet from the bull, ignoring the glares from the art patrons. He knelt and examined it, working his fingers in under the edge and lifting it with a grunt. "Where's attack dog when he would be useful?" He slid the heavy metal out of the way, and set back on the brickwork. He looked down the hole, then up at me. "You want to go first?"

"So the monsters can get me first?"

He opened his mouth, paused, then grinned at me again. "What, is that our thing now?"

I sat down at the edge of the hole, my legs dangling into it, and held my hands out to him. "Just lower me down so I don't fall on my ass."

He took my hands, his grip tight, and helped me slide down into the hole, then let go once I had my feet settled. I took a step away and he followed me in. He pulled the map Virgil had given us out of the inner pocket of his jacket, held it up, and examined it in the light coming in from above it.

"It looks like we need to follow the tunnel up to our right."

I took a look and then called the whispers. They brushed against my shoulders, figures curling down my arms while the shadows pooled at my feet. When I asked them which way, they agreed with Ranger.

"Good news," I said. "You're right."

"I feel like I'm right a lot of the time," he said, as we started off. The tunnels here were wider than the ones we had followed to find the Gorgon, and we were able to walk side by side as we went. Still not a lot of headroom, though. Ranger pulled out his phone, turning on the flashlight so we could see where we were going because it didn't take long to lose any light we had from where we entered.

"You didn't bring your bat," I said.

"How would I carry it on the bike? And from what Virgil said, it's one monster. I think we can handle it."

Our voices were echoing down the tunnel. I lowered the volume to a whisper. "The Gorgon was one monster."

Ranger followed my example. "Yeah, but Virgil said they were telling you this one would be easy. They ever been wrong before?"

I paused to think about it. The information they had given me hadn't been wrong, but the Furies weren't above making mistakes. And what memories they were managing to resurrect might not be the whole story.

"I don't know," I finally said, choosing to be honest.

"Real confidence-booster there."

I shrugged. "I'm operating in the dark here."

"That feels more like a modus operandi for you. Do you ever come into the light?"

Our steps were echoing off the walls, too. There hadn't been any rain in a while, so the tunnels were mostly dry with occasional puddles of water. The noise was making me itch. "Do you ever have conversations that stay surface level?" I asked him because in spite of the fact that I didn't want to draw attention from anything that was down here I can't stay quiet.

"I like to know what makes people tick."

The figures were refraining from scratching at things for a change, choosing to stay against me, fingers curled up and down my arms, the shadows spilling out and flowing along with us as we walked, the whispers sighing in my ears.

"Is that why you were so pushy?" I asked.

"Pushy?" he asked. "When? When we met?" He had turned his head to look at me rather than where he was going.

"You can include that as part of it, yeah."

"Pushy," he muttered. "Yeah, I guess I was pushy." He ruffled his hair and went silent for a moment. "Honestly, whole truth here?"

"Yes," I said. I wasn't sure I wanted to hear it, but Ranger can't always hear the lies I tell.

"I was curious about you to start with," he said. "But that night at the apartment fire when Greg said 'That's not where I left you,' well, that made me worried."

"Worried?"

He stopped turning fully toward me, one hand on my arm so I was forced to stop or shake him off. "You can't tell me the kind of impression someone would get from that wouldn't be what it was."

"I don't know what kind of impression you got," I pointed out, although I had an inkling.

He snorted. "Stop being obtuse. You can't tell me that didn't come off as Greg being—" he paused, like he was rethinking how he wanted to say it. "He was angry."

I couldn't step back from him here because there wasn't enough space, but I twitched my arm, and he dropped his hand. "He was mad at *you*," I said.

"Yeah, I know that now," he said. "But I come in, and he's constantly blocking people from you, and looming, and telling you what to do, where to go, making decisions for you whenever Virgil wasn't overriding shit. He was constantly on top of you, and I couldn't figure out if it was because you were a danger to yourself, or if he was a danger to you."

"He's never been a danger to me," I said.

Ranger made a frustrated noise. "I'm not saying he is, but that's how he came across. Not all heroes are good people when they're off the clock."

"Wouldn't that mean they're not good people when they're on the clock either?"

"Some of them put on a good show for the cameras," he said plainly. "How was I supposed to know he wasn't that kind? That he wasn't the reason your knee pops like that?"

I flared up. "He had nothing—"

"I know! Jesus, Meg. Your response was that you're just clumsy. You don't know how someone might take that? What they might hear when you automatically blame yourself for injuries?"

I opened my mouth, shut it, and thought about it for a minute. "Oh," I finally said. I didn't want to ask how that might have been the conclusion he jumped to because I had just been me, all sarcasm and deflection, and I didn't think my answers through before I gave them. I had just been trying to discourage him from talking to me at all. I needed to back out of this conversation before it went somewhere I regretted.

The silence was also quickly reaching the uncomfortable threshold for me, so I cleared my throat. "We should go find this thing and get back."

He was quiet for another beat. "You know this isn't the end of this conversation."

"I don't see why it's not," I said, starting down the tunnel again so that he was either going to have to come with me or make me walk through the dark.

He chose to follow me, and we came to a fork. He checked the map again. "This says left."

No, the whispers said. I headed down the right tunnel.

"Meg!" He came trotting after me. "Do you have to shut down like that?"

"That's your question? Not where am I going?"

"I trust you to know what you're doing."

"You think Greg doesn't trust me to—" I started, bristling.

"I think he lets his need to keep you protected override

common sense," Ranger said pointedly. "This isn't an attack on either of you."

"Fine," I said. "Can we go kill this thing and forget I ever asked?"

"No," he said.

"You're going to leave the monster wandering around?"

"That's not what I meant, and you know it."

The volume of our voices had been creeping up as we were continuing down the tunnel, and it was echoing off the walls again, making me wince.

"Can we please leave it?" I hissed.

"No," he said again. "You keep almost dying, and I'm going to regret it if I don't get this off my chest."

"Nope. No, you do not get to—" I started shouting.

"Not like that!" he roared back. "I mean, yes, at first, damn it," he swore, turned away from me, and then turning back. "I don't have a lot of friends. You're a friend."

"That's all I better be," I said.

"No offense, but I'm not fucking up what Maniac and I have going for you."

"She would just set you on fire if you tried."

"Maniac is not as murdery as you are. She talks things out before she tries resorting to violence."

"Glad I manage to out villain the villain."

"You certainly give it your maximum effort," he said smirking at me.

It made me feel better to know we were back on solid footing here. "I don't give maximum effort to much of anything."

"You take things to extremes all the time," he said. "Case in point—"

"Excuse me, but I'm pretty sure you said friendship is not where it started." Oh, damn it, I just led us back into it.

"No, it's not," he said softly. "I definitely had a lot of – interest – in you that way. But then I got to know you."

I couldn't help it: I grinned at him. "What, my winning

personality wasn't a turn on for you?"

He laughed. "No, you're – look, you're difficult."

"Tell me something I don't know."

"I'm trying to! You keep sidetracking the conversation."

"Because we're wasting time when we should be hunting down a monster."

"This is how I know you and Greg are a good match," he said. "You're both too single-minded."

"Thought you thought we weren't serious."

"I knew you for all of five minutes when I said that."

"Oh, so you're saying you were wrong?"

"Is that what you want to hear? Because unlike some people, I don't have a problem admitting when I'm wrong."

"Greg apologizes to me all the time."

Ranger snorted. "Yeah, but does he do it just so you'll stop arguing with him?"

"Maybe," I said.

"Okay, look, you're sidetracking us again. My mom moved us around a lot when I was a kid. I didn't get to make friends for long because by the time I had any we were moving again. I kept it up when I got out on my own. This is literally the longest I've stayed in one place."

I didn't have anything I could say to that. It sounded lonely.

I know I didn't have any friends or social life really when I was on my own, but at least I had a home.

He sighed. "Don't give me that look. I know that look."

"What look?" I said.

"It's your 'I don't know that I want to know where this is going' look. You do it a lot. I'm not asking you to be my therapist. Just, you're important to me. All of you are."

"I think I want to know why you chose now, of all times, to make this kind of confession."

"We have a tendency to go off and do our own thing when we're not saving the world," he said. "How often do all five of us hang out?"

"Thought we should have things outside of each other? And what do you call movie night?"

"You know what I meant, and those don't count. Could you just make the confession less difficult instead of more?"

"That wouldn't be on brand," I said.

"You—" he started, then paused shaking his head. "Just don't fucking die on this mission. Greg will never let me live it down."

I was silent.

"What?" he said. "What?"

"I don't know that he would recover enough to—" and I paused, unsure of what I wanted to say.

"Yeah," he said. "As humor, it doesn't go over well."

At this point, we both fell silent, me following the tug of the whispers, Ranger keeping pace with me while we wove deeper in.

"Are they going to lead us back out?" Ranger asked eventually, "because I don't have a way to mark where we've been going."

"You can't tell me that phone doesn't have somewhere to jot down notes."

"I've been using it so we can see where we're going."

"Greg's going to be mad at both of us if we got lost because we were busy talking."

"Try not to throw me under the bus for—" he started when a bellow echoed its way up the tunnel towards us.

The Minotaur had found us, and it was charging. The whispers howled, the figures and shadows slamming into him as soon as he had hit my range. He bellowed again, stumbling backwards, shaking his head, but the way he did it, it traveled down from his head to his shoulders.

So, you know how often the Minotaur is portrayed in media as this hulking beast? That his body mass matches the bull part of him?

Yeah, no, this was nothing like that. He looked more shrunken. His bull head was somewhere around the size of a calf's, and his body was quite clearly human, but thin, a noticeable lack of muscle overall. The most impressive part of him were the horns. They were similar to a Texan longhorn's. I wasn't sure how he managed to get in and out of the sewers with things that size, but even they were spindly in appearance.

But the whispers had been right, he was easy to take down. In the end, the hunt for him was anticlimactic because the figures and shadows tore him apart in seconds.

Ranger and I stared at the remains for a moment. "Well," he said, "how do we get back?"

"I'm not the one with the map."

He snorted and started back the way we came. "You're lucky I have a good sense of direction."

CHAPTER FIVE

"I think we need another team building exercise,"
Ranger told me, as he helped pull me up out of the manhole.
We had been down there long enough that the late afternoon
sunlight was slanting across the plaza, casting long shadows
along the artwork. It was still busy though, crowded with
people who eyed us curiously. I mean, even in Malus you don't
have heroes popping out of the sewers every day.

"Camping again?" I asked warily. Not because it hadn't
been a good experience, but it had ended with a visit from Hera,
and I didn't want to know who else would decide to show up
while we were by a body of water.

"Did you even see a bear?" Ranger asked.

"No," I said, standing up. "But that doesn't mean next
time—"

Something hit me in the chest, hard enough to knock me
back and off my feet.

"Fuck! Meg, Meg, look at me!" Ranger was leaning over
me; people were screaming and running. Something clanged off
the metal sculpture of the bull. I must have had a no awareness
minute when I got hit because I was leaning back against the
sculpture itself. Ranger must have yanked me up and gotten us
behind it. My chest hurt; just breathing was painful.

Something hit the bricks to my right sending red shards

of clay up.

Ranger was pulling the zipper on my jacket down, and I knocked his hand away. "Damn it, Meg, I have to make sure you don't have a bullet in your chest again!" he snapped at me.

"The whispers would be a lot angrier if I did," I wheezed. They were angry, yes, but willing to wait until I brought them out right now instead of raging.

There was another clang. Ranger automatically ducked his head down. "Fuck. Who the fuck is shooting at us?"

"I'll do you one better," I said, still wheezing. "Why are they shooting at us?"

"You're going to try and one up me right now?" He had pulled out his phone, had it up to his ear. "Jesus, does attack dog – Greg! Apollo Square, someone's trying to shoot Meg!" There was another clang, and Ranger moved forward, huddling his body over mine.

"So, how long are we going to hide?" I asked. I wanted to squirm away, but Ranger had his arms around me, blocking me from doing something stupid like getting shot just because I didn't want to be touched. Also, I wasn't sure I could get up for long anyway.

"I don't feel like getting shot by something that high caliber. I can't stretch the perimeter far enough to figure out where he's sniping from before I get hit."

The ground behind me shook.

"Seriously, it's for the dramatic effect isn't it?" Ranger asked.

The sound the bullet made when it hit Greg was a kind of—thump, and then I heard it hit the bricks with a clink.

I heard him take off again, and then distantly, a scream. Ranger backed up so that he wasn't leaning right up against me. He poked his head around the statue, and I plucked at his arm. "Don't do that. What if he's not dead yet?"

He pulled his head back. "I feel like it's pretty safe at this point."

A clang off the bull proved him wrong.

"Fuck!" he said, ducking back down. "How has Greg not killed him?"

"Maybe there's more than one?"

More bricks shattered.

"How many more than one?" Ranger said. "You would think they would get while the getting is good before Greg figures out where they are."

"Should we move?" I asked.

"No, just stay down."

"What about all the other people who are here?"

Ranger took a chance to peek out and around the statue. He ducked back just in time because a bullet went through the air where his face had been to hit the bricks just beyond us. "You know, I think we're the only target they're after."

Greg landed next to us. "It's Mirage."

"What?" I said. "What is he shooting at me for?!"

"I'd like to ask him that myself," Greg growled, "before I rip him apart."

"Is it because I insulted his art?"

"Is this more need-to-know shit Virgil wouldn't tell me about?" Ranger asked.

"Why isn't he dead yet?" I asked Greg.

"I got stuck in his fucking illusion. Took me a minute to get out, and now I've got to recalculate what the trajectory is."

"You got stuck in it?"

"He had it set up to cover the room. He screamed and ran from me, and then I hit it."

"He must've camped out for a while if he's set up with more than one nest," Ranger said.

Greg poked his head around, and I didn't even see the bullet, until it hit the bricks as a flattened circle. Greg was rubbing his forehead, pulling his head back behind the statue. "Ow," he said. "He went up a floor."

"Great. Take me with you," I said.

"No," Greg and Ranger said at the same time.

"Trust me," I said.

"I am not—" Greg argued.

"Take her," Ranger said.

"What?" Greg turned on him. "That's—"

"Trust her," Ranger said. "Tell her what floor she needs to be on, then keep him distracted. I'm going to buy you time to get up there without him realizing you've left shelter."

He darted away from us, toward one of the other statues. A puff of brick appeared behind him as a bullet hit the ground at his heels.

"God damn it," Greg swore, but he snatched me up and shot into the air, landing us on the roof of a building with a clear view of the plaza below. He yanked up a trapdoor set in the concrete, tossing it away from us. There was a ladder to the floor below. "You need to go down ten floors," he said, his eyes searching mine.

"I'm going to break the illusion," I said. "That's all. He won't even know I'm there until it's too late."

"He said his illusions hold up even through death—" Greg protested.

"Yeah, back when I wasn't at full power," I said. "He doesn't stand a chance now."

"Watch yourself," Greg said gruffly.

"Always," I said with a smile. I gave him a kiss, turned and slid my way down the ladder.

I was up at the top of the elevators, the mechanisms for their motors and lifts evenly spaced out in a long row from one end of the room to the other. I made my way to the door across from me. It was unlocked.

You know, I really get lucky that way sometimes.

Mirage had said his illusions would hold up even under death, but he hadn't reckoned on having to deal with a god. Plus I think he meant the death of the subject that the illusion was on. He hadn't mentioned what would happen if he dies.

The other question: was it definitely Mirage this time? Or had he paid someone off again?

The whispers, figures, shadows and I were going to find

out. I pulled them to me, and we set off down the stairwell the door opened onto. The figures were flowing along the walls, their long fingers brushing along the floor as we went. The shadows went spilling with us, pooling over the stairs, and in my ears the whispers giggled.

When we had counted down ten floors, we opened the door.

The hallway looked normal – tan walls, beige carpet – could be an office in any building in any city. Fake fern plants set on either side of the elevator doors.

We stepped forward, the shadows rising up at my back, swaying. The whispers tugged at me, and I followed them, until we came to a door past the elevators, about halfway down the hall. They were hissing in my ears now. Slowly, we twisted the knob; we wanted to get in silently so we didn't attract his attention until we were ready.

We pushed the door open gently, centimeters at a time, until we could peek our head in.

The room was empty: one long length of more beige carpet and walls, not even office furniture. The only thing of interest to see were the windows at the other end from us.

Here, the whispers said.

The windows were more than ten feet away from us.

We slid into the room, slowly sliding the door shut behind us, and then I let the figures and shadows expand, watching the way the shadows billowed up and over the furniture that was there that I couldn't see.

I ducked down behind what had looked like a desk from the way they swirled around it, pulling them back to me in case Mirage moved and hit the wall of fear before I could get close enough for a quick take down.

He would sense the unease in the air soon enough.

I heard the crack of a gunshot, the sound as he chambered another round. I sent the figures and shadows out again, watching as they rose up to try and flow over another desk before I pulled them back.

It wasn't long before my legs were aching from moving in that crouched, stealthy manner. I had only made it halfway across the room, but I was almost within range of the windows.

I tripped over a chair I hadn't noticed even with the shadows' and figures' rippling bodies outlining the furniture.

It crashed to the floor – it was one of those rolling computer chairs, and my foot had caught under the pronged leg in the worst possible epic klutz manner. I scrambled away from it, knocking another chair out of the way, and ducked down behind a desk. The figures and shadows surged outward to the edge of my range because I heard the noise at the window.

Mirage knew I was here.

"Oh, hey, Meg," he called. "Your shadow friends are – bigger than they used to be."

I didn't say anything because I didn't want to give him my exact location when I couldn't see where he was.

"Bet you're wondering why I'm doing this," he said. "I mean, it's not just because you broke my nose."

From what I recall, he did that to himself, unintentional as it was at the moment. But I wasn't going to tell him to stop monologuing until I could figure out how to get closer without getting shot again.

"This is about revenge, on you and all your associates. Not for the nose, though, man, just want to clarify that."

Oh my God, get to the damn point.

He stopped talking long enough to take a potshot out the window and chamber another round.

"No man, this is about the fact that you – or maybe Fortress? – spilled the beans about me. Doesn't really matter which one of you did it because won't it just break his heart when I shoot you in the face? This is about you assholes blowing my cover after I helped you."

From what I recall, we very specifically did not blow his cover. Although I definitely wanted to.

"Do you have any idea—" and this time I heard the cracking clang as he shot one of the desks, and then chambered another round, "what those assholes tried to do to me when they found out I wasn't dead?" I heard the tread as he headed away from the window; it sounded like he was going down to the right of the room.

From what I had seen, these desks were set up in militaristic rows, so eventually he was going to come to my row and have a clear shot.

Maybe I could talk him down.

Look, stop laughing, this isn't funny. You never know. He might stop long enough to listen.

"Hey, Mirage," I called, hoping even with me speaking it would take him a minute to locate me. "It wasn't us, but I will absolutely help you hunt down whoever it was if you promise not to shoot me in the face."

"Oh, yeah, like I'm going to believe you," he said.

"You honestly think Vigilante would've let us go blabbing about where you were when he could just keep blackmailing you?" At this point I just wanted him distracted long enough that Greg could locate him on sound alone.

"You know, I would say you have a point, man, but I feel like you're lying to me. You were pretty pissed about the whole 'faking my own death' thing."

"You could've just asked me to murder you," I yelled out.

"You know the illusions can cover sounds too, right? Whatever you're trying to communicate to Fortress out there, he can't hear you."

Well fuck.

But could it cover messages? Who would I owe the least to if I called them?

Or I could wait and charge him when he came to my row. As long as I stayed out of the way of the chairs, I might be able to get far enough before he could get a shot off. Or hope that if he did manage to shoot me, whatever portion of the suit he hit still had enough integrity that I wouldn't die.

Starting position it was.

I waited, muscles tensed, because he would either be stupid enough to announce his location, or I was about to get shot in the face.

"There you are," he said, and I sprang forward, the figures and shadows flying with me, the whispers howling in my ears, and he took a startled step backwards. It was all the hesitation they needed as they slammed into him, knocking him down. I went with them and kicked him in the ribs. At least, it felt like I hit him in the ribs.

He screamed, and I could hear the sounds of fumbling as the figures clawed at him. I reached down and yanked at the stock of the rifle, trying to make sure the muzzle was pointed away from me.

He let go of the gun and I staggered back, clutching it to my chest and panting.

The figures and shadows had him pinned to the floor, but they weren't ripping at him anymore. They were billowing around him, and he was curled up into a ball, quivering. The illusion gone, I could see the furniture around me. The desks were those old metal ones, the rolling chairs the lightweight cheap ones. More fake ferns.

The whispers were in my ears. *What shall we do with this one?*

I had a choice. Greg would choose to believe it had been self-defense if I told him it was because if I let Mirage go, he would just come after me again. Virgil might know the truth of it, but he would also assume the choice the Furies just gave me wasn't a real one because they were vengeance, and they had ignored me before.

But did I want to out villain the villain?

I pulled out my phone and called Virgil. He answered on the first ring.

"Meg," he said.

"Mirage says hi," I told him.

"Where are you?"

"Um, good question. Building off Apollo Square. You

might need to ask Fortress which one exactly, I wasn't paying attention."

If Mirage had been coming after me just to come after me, the figures and shadows would've ripped him apart the moment they hit him. But someone had gotten a hold of information only Virgil, Greg and I were aware of. Well, Maniac too, but she had said she wasn't going to tell on him, and I believed her.

"Maniac and I are on the way," Virgil said and hung up.

"Hey, so I'm going to do you a solid, and not tell Fortress you did, in fact, shoot me," I told Mirage.

He whimpered. "Can you—" he said, his voice shaking, "Can you pull them off me or something?"

"Hmm, no," I said, leaning back against a desk as I placed another call.

"Meg!" Ranger said. "What the fuck is going on?"

"Hey, so is Fortress still in the air?"

"That—" Ranger started, "No, he's down next to me. Fucker took a potshot and still managed to hit me."

"What?" I said. "Where? I've got him down; I'll rip off whatever limb he hit."

Mirage whimpered again, a quivering ball on the floor. "No man! I swear, I'm sorry!"

"It's just a flesh wound."

"Yeah, you got any limbs left?"

"If you're quoting random movie references at me, I'm not going to get it," he sighed. "Greg took off and is headed your way."

Greg came in through the window and slammed desks out of his way, snarling.

The whispers, figures, shadows and I stood our ground.

"Get them out of my way," Greg said.

"No," we said.

"Meg—"

"Guardian," we said, our black eyes fixed on his brown. "This is our will."

I saw the moment on Greg's face, when he realized, truly realized, what I am.

Despite our encounters with the others, despite what Virgil has told him, I don't think Greg really believed that my power is as ancient as the world itself.

Not that they can remember it yet.

"I did not think you could get any creepier, but somehow you did, man," Mirage said from the floor.

∞

Ranger came up to the floor before Virgil and Maniac had made it to our location, so the three of us had waited in uncomfortable silence while Mirage stayed cowering on the floor.

Virgil came striding in alone. "Meg," he said.

I looked over at him and let the whispers go. I could see the way he instantly relaxed, but he stayed all business, coming over to Mirage and me.

Ranger stood by Greg. "Where's Maniac?" he asked.

"In the Hummer," Virgil said. "I asked her to keep an eye on the vehicles. So, Mirage, what's the occasion for the visit?"

Mirage hadn't gotten up from the floor; the farthest he had moved was to sit up with his back against the wall. He pointed a finger at me. "She told someone."

"No, I didn't," I snapped. I saw the way Greg relaxed when he heard the truth in my words.

"If it wasn't you, man, it was Fortress," Mirage said accusingly. "One of you assholes—"

"Enough," Virgil said. "It wasn't either of them. It wasn't anyone on this team because I would know." Virgil had a hand up on his chin; he looked over at me. "What happened?"

"He tried to shoot me," I said. Greg had a hand in his hair; he was on the tips of his toes, poised. I moved off the desk and stepped over to him. He dropped to his heels, and when I stepped up to him, he looked relieved and wrapped his arms around me.

"Look, man, I said sorry," Mirage said.

"Only because I said I was going to rip one of your limbs off," I muttered. Greg's chest rumbled under me when he chuckled.

Virgil ignored the exchange. "Explain why you would think Fortress and Vengeance exposed you in the first place."

"The others came after me," Mirage said. "A few weeks ago. Flayer showed up at my house, and it's a good thing he's an idiot, but look, man," he was shaking back a sleeve, exposing his arm to show a sunken, shiny, pink area. "Asshole took off a whole chunk."

"How'd you get away?" Virgil asked.

"Dude's scared of spiders. I had them coming out of his ears. It was fucking hilarious, man." At the look the four of us gave him, he cleared his throat. "Anyway, that's when I ran. Someone talked, and if it wasn't you, I owe whoever it was."

"Hmm," Virgil said. "Well, it wasn't one of us, so we can't help you. You three ready to go?"

"Wait! Wait, man, look, help me track them down and take them out. I'll pay you."

"We're not mercenaries," Greg said.

"You'd be doing the world a favor," Mirage said, wheedling. "Hero work you get paid extra for. There's no way this wasn't one of the villains. And I heard you say Maniac. They'll be coming after her eventually. You might as well get paid for getting rid of them before they become a problem for you."

"We'll see what we can find." Virgil said. "I'll send you our billable hours. Now if you'll excuse us—"

"Wait! Come on, man, I need protection. You can't just leave me here!"

"That costs extra," Virgil said.

"I'm good for it!"

Virgil was silent for a moment. "Fine, get up."

"You're—" Greg protested.

"Yes, I am," Virgil said, and then he loomed over Mirage. "If you attack either me or anyone else on my team, or use any of your illusions on them, I will end you."

Mirage cringed back. "Yeah, man, got it."

"Good," Virgil said. "Follow me."

All of us followed his order and trailed after him out and down the stairwell to street level. I think he chose that over trapping everyone in an elevator when Greg was glowering. When we got out, Maniac was leaning against the Hummer parked at the curb. Ranger's bike was parked behind it.

"When did you move my bike?" he asked.

"When we got here," Maniac told him. "Virgil said watch the vehicles. I wasn't going to leave yours in the plaza."

"Thanks," he said.

"You're welcome." She looked Mirage over. "What's with Shaggy?"

"Client," Virgil said. "Maniac, meet Mirage."

"He's Mirage?" Maniac said, one eyebrow raised.

"You're leaving out part of the introductions, man," Mirage said.

"Shut up and get in the car," Virgil said.

"Alright, damn," he muttered, pulling open the passenger side door and climbing in past Maniac.

"Ranger, if we can load your bike into the back, I would like you and Maniac to ride with me," Virgil said. Greg stepped around us, opened the back of the Hummer and picked Ranger's bike up and swung it in.

"Don't scratch the paint!" Ranger said.

Greg shot him a look, set the bike down inside the car, and closed the back up.

Virgil came up to us, "Fortress, if you could take Vengeance back the usual way? Take the time you need to check for any injuries. Call me if there's been any permanent damage."

Greg's face paled, and he knelt, shoving my jacket up out his way and pressing his ear to my stomach, his arms wrapped around my thighs so that I couldn't step back. I grabbed at his shoulders automatically, but he wouldn't have let me fall. I felt his fingers tighten briefly, and then he sighed.

"We're good," he said. "Just as strong as it was this morning."

"We're attracting attention," Virgil said. "You might want to get up and go unless you want this moment to end up on the news. The press will have a field day with theories."

"I feel like they would be pushing the one theory," I said, but Greg stood and lifted me up, launching us into the air.

He went slow enough that it took us the same amount of time to get back to the Tower as it would've if we had just ridden with Virgil. When we finally landed on the balcony, he insisted on opening the door, poking his head in and listening before he would let me go in.

When he finally let me go into our apartment, I unzipped my jacket and heard the metal clink when it hit our floor. I winced.

"You didn't tell me he had actually shot you," Greg said. He came up behind me, slid the jacket down my arms and pulled at my shirt. "Arms up."

It hurt to raise them, and when I winced again, Greg gently pushed my arms back down and tore the shirt apart up the back.

"Hey!" I protested. "I think there was another option other than destroying it." But I shed the shredded shirt off the front of me without having to lift my arms.

"Noted," Greg said, unzipping the catsuit, and peeling it down just far enough that he could see the giant bruise across my chest. "Would you rather I go rip him apart?"

"So you take it out on my shirt?"

"Yes," Greg said. He worked the suit down enough that it was hanging off my waist. "God damn it, what kind of caliber did he hit you with?"

"You got shot too. You tell me."

He snorted, scooped me back up and marched me over to the bed, settling me against the pillows. "Compress, Arnica. No complaining." He disappeared into the bathroom.

"What happened with your Minotaur?" I called to him.

"I got to take out two of them," he said, coming back out of the bathroom and setting the compress across my chest.

"You're not bloody," I said.

"I broke their necks. They weren't much of a challenge."

Well, that matched what the whispers had told me.

He was watching me seriously. "Meg, we need to talk."

My heart sped up. "Do we have to?"

He put a hand on my face, his thumb brushing my cheek. "It's not a bad talk."

"I already got stuck having a heart-to-heart with Ranger today. I don't know that I can handle more talks."

He paused. "What kind of heart-to-heart?"

"A 'he's totally over me but we're important to him' heart-to-heart."

Greg snorted. "He is not over you. I can hear it. He just thinks he is."

"Wouldn't that be the same thing?"

"No," Greg said. "There's this river in Egypt—"

"I know this joke," I said.

He smiled at me and moved so he was leaning back against the pillows with me, his arm tucked behind me so that I was snug against his side. I relaxed into him, his body warm where it pressed against me. His casual affection with me had become familiar, comforting.

I had never expected to have that with anyone.

He kissed the top of my head. "Which part of you is Meg, and which part is them?"

"I'm not sure," I said, honestly. "None of the others work the way we do."

"Sometimes it seems like you answer together, and

sometimes it's you, alone."

"When?" I asked. "All the time?"

"Yes. Like now, it's just us, you're the one answering me. But there are times, even when you're not calling on them, that I can hear them in your voice."

"Does it bother you?" I asked, unsure of whether I wanted to know the answer.

"No," he said. "I knew. I knew you were different." He scrubbed at his face. "I just didn't know the why or how."

"Hmm," I said, settling my head against his chest, and closing my eyes.

"We're not done," he said, giving me a poke in my side. "What is a Guardian?"

"They can't remember," I said without opening my eyes, "but Hera has one."

"Still not done."

"Now what?"

"We're going back a step. Why didn't you tell me Mirage shot you?"

I lifted my head. "I didn't want you to murder him yet."

"Don't hide these things from me."

"Technically, Ranger lied first."

"I'm not married to Ranger," he said, "and you should stop shoving him under the bus when you go along with his stupid plans. You should've told me the truth."

My face flushed, and I looked down. "Virgil told me what happened to Grenadier wasn't necessary to end the threat. I was worried you would kill Mirage before we could find out why he came after me to start with."

Greg opened his mouth, paused, and shut it, his jaw clenched and lips thin. "I would've, if you hadn't stood in the way."

"We can always kill him, after we find out who figured out he wasn't dead."

Greg chuckled. "No, at that point it's just straight up murder. I can't do that."

"Good."

He looked me in the eye. "Good?"

"You're not vengeance," I said. "I don't want you to be."

He kissed me, his hands on my waist, inching higher. I pulled the compress off my chest and tossed it away. I heard it hit the floor.

"Meg," he said, and my heart fluttered, but he was letting go of me, sliding off the bed to retrieve the compress from the floor. He disappeared into the bathroom again, then came out and climbed back onto the bed with me. He set the reheated compress on my chest.

"Seriously?" I said.

"Yes, seriously," he said, settling back next to me, pulling me against his side again. He kissed the side of my head. "Sleep. I know you were falling asleep once already."

I snorted, settled my head against his chest and closed my eyes.

CHAPTER SIX

I could hear crying.

Piercing, it wailed, but as hard as I searched, I couldn't find the source.

By the time the crib appeared, I was running frantically back and forth.

It was just sitting there in our living room, where nothing had been before.

The cry was emanating from it, and at first, I was relieved.

When I went up to it, it was just a baby, its face screwed up, mouth gaping.

Until it opened its eyes.

I staggered back, tripped, and fell onto the floor, still facing the crib.

It turned its head, staring at me between the bars with those red, red eyes.

∞

"Meg!" The voice was shaking, a hand trembling against my shoulder. "Meg, wake up."

The whispers were there, sighing in my ears, quiet and calm, and once I had opened my eyes to stare up at the dark ceiling they vanished.

Greg slid an arm under me, lifting me up into a sitting position as he settled me back against him, my head on his chest. "Nightmare?" he asked, although he knew the answer.

"Yes," I whispered. His arm tightened around me.

"Do you want to talk about it?"

I shook my head, burying my face against him. I could feel the tears start.

"Shhh," he said, his nose in my hair. He brought his other hand up and set it against my back while I clung to him, sniffling and willing the tears away.

His phone rang, and it made me jump.

He sighed, picked it up off the bedside table, answered it. "Detective White."

You know, none of us ever just say "hello."

That made me lift my head up. Greg straightened up as well, pulling his arm out from behind me as he moved to get off the bed.

"How many?" he asked. "The remains, were they the same as—" He was pacing now. "No, we found more than one, but we may have missed some. We'll search again. Do you need us to come to the scene?" He had paused in his pacing, his back to me, one hand in his hair. "No, no, we'll make sure it's taken care of. Call me if the medical examiner finds anything different about these teeth marks." He hung up.

"What?" I asked, although I already knew.

"There were three this time," he said. "Roommates."

I slid off the bed, wiggling my way out of my jeans and the catsuit, headed to the dresser to grab clean clothes.

"What are you doing?" Greg asked me.

"Getting dressed," I said slowly.

He snorted. "I can see that. You should be resting."

I pulled on clean clothes. "I'm fine. The baby is fine. I think I can at least come downstairs with you to talk to Virgil."

He sighed and got my outfit free of my jeans from where I had left it unceremoniously tossed on the floor. "Fine. I have

to bring this to Virgil anyway. He's going to have to replace it."
He stepped up to me and put a hand on my face. "You
shouldn't go out in the field until you have a new one."

"Okay," I said.

He looked relieved, gave me a kiss, and moved his hand
from my face down to my hand. "Come on, let's get this over
with."

We headed out the door, down the stairs and up the
hallway, and Greg knocked on Virgil's door. There was a pause,
then the sound of the locks flipping, and the door creaked
open.

"In the study," Virgil's voice floated out to us.

We headed in and found Virgil seated on the floor cross-
legged, open books spread in a half circle in front of him, one
on his lap as he leaned over, running a finger down the page of
a book on the floor.

'What are you doing?" I asked.

"No one, for they are many," Virgil said. He pinched
the bridge of his nose, rubbed his eyes. "I don't see anything in
any information I have on Minotaurs that mentions 'no one.'
I'm trying to track down what it could refer to." He looked up
from the books. "What brings you here at this midnight hour?"

"Detective White called. They have more victims," Greg
said.

"How many?" Virgil asked, his tone sharp.

"Three, roommates."

Virgil reached forward and snagged one of the other
books, pulling it to him. "Did we miss something? Or did we
not find all of them?" He was quiet for a moment, his eyes
following his finger as it ran it across the page, then he looked
back up at us. "Does White need you on scene? Is she still at
the scene?"

"She was when we hung up."

"Go there, and take Meg."

"Her suit is compromised," Greg said, holding out the
catsuit, "and we already know at least one villain had it out for

her just today."

Virgil made an irritated noise. "Meg, did you get shot and not tell anyone?"

"I feel like you know the answer to that question," I said.

Virgil focused on me, his lips twitching. "Touché."

"For what it's worth, Ranger started the ball rolling on that one."

The corner of Virgil's eyes crinkled. "I don't think he'll appreciate you throwing him under the bus yet again."

"It's the same bus."

"Hmm. I believe you're wasting time. Greg, you need to take Meg with you. Call White back and make sure she's still at the scene."

Greg didn't move. "She needs something. I'm not taking her out completely unprotected."

The look on Virgil's face softened, an expression I had never seen him make before. "I understand your concern, but she will be with you. If she's not safe with you, who is she safe with?"

"You," Greg said without hesitation.

Virgil looked back down at the books. "Touched, I'm sure. But we need what they can tell Meg before more people die."

I expected Greg to protest again, but he simply set the suit down on the floor in front of Virgil's books, came back and steered me out the door. When I turned my face up to look at his, he had that relieved look again, and we were barely in the hallway before I spoke.

"What? What did you hear?"

"Come on, we've got to get going."

"But what—" I said, but he had pulled out his phone already and was hitting the call button. I scowled at him.

"Are you still at the scene?" he asked when White answered. At least, I assume she answered and he wasn't just pretending to talk to her. He could and I would never know since I wouldn't be able to hear her. "Yes, Vengeance and I are on the way. We need to see it while it's intact." A pause. "Yes. Be there in, five?" He hung up and scooped me up even though we weren't in our own hall yet.

"If you think carrying me the rest of the way is going to distract me, you're wrong," I told him.

He grunted.

"What did you hear?" I repeated.

Greg had us out on our balcony before he answered. He brushed some of my curls out of my face, his hand settling in its usual spot, with his thumb brushing my cheek. "We're family, and he'll protect you too," he said, before he leapt us into the air.

∞

We went back to the brownstone district.

I mean, it's not actually called that. It's just that it's got rows and rows of shoulder-to-shoulder brown brick buildings all built around the 1800s. The first of the tract housing, even though the quality of these buildings is probably better than the tract homes of today.

They don't build them like they used to.

The one we landed in front of looked just like all the others; the only difference was what kind of flowers were in the window boxes.

Or in this case, no flowers. The window boxes were empty, even of dirt. Guess the tenants weren't green thumbed kind of people.

The sidewalks were also empty, no onlookers here in the middle of the night. Although maybe they had already been and gone, tired of the non-action.

The CSI and coroner vans were parked at the curb. The coroner and his assistant were standing by the railing, arguing with White. She had a finger in the coroner's face, her face flushed and shiny. Her braids had come loose from their coiled bun, and she was distinctly making her point.

"You can collect the remains when I say we're done with the scene, and we're not done with the scene."

"We've been standing here for three hours!" The coroner was shouting back, making no attempt to keep his voice modulated like White was.

"And I told you—"

But whatever she had told the coroner Greg wasn't interested in because he stepped up, looming. "Is there a problem?"

The coroner started to turn and appeal his case to Greg until he realized who was standing there. Even if someone doesn't recognize who Greg is to start with, when he gets that look on his face, most people do a double take and back off.

"Fortress," White said, sounding both relieved and irritated. "Vengeance," she said, addressing me with a friendlier tone.

I don't get how I'm the one the cops like. Greg's the public face. Virgil makes him be the one to deal with the press. He says it's because when Greg wants to be, he's affable, whereas I am "too never" (whatever that means), Ranger is too smug, and Maniac is too controversial.

When I asked him why he didn't want to deal with the press, he had pretended not to hear the question.

Before White could say anything else, however, Greg sighed and did an about face. I half-turned to see what had attracted his attention.

The cameraman who had tried to sneak up and catch some footage turned tail and ran.

I snickered.

"Vengeance," Greg said.

"Fortress," I mocked.

Greg's lips twitched.

White, the coroner and his assistant were watching us.

"Is she always like this?" White finally asked.

"Yes," Greg said, but he was smiling at me. He wrapped an arm around my waist, drawing me against him.

"You're going to give them footage," I said.

"Let them look," he said, turning to White. "Where are the remains?"

"In the bedrooms," she said, heading inside. The coroner and his assistant started to trail along behind us. "Excuse you," White said to them. "Private party." She paused at the door and turned back to us. "Watch out for the footprints." Then she went inside.

We followed her in, up the stairs just past the front door. It was set up exactly like the first brownstone we had been to, but White led us to the first bedroom just off the landing on the second floor. "This is the first set."

Again, the bedding was so soaked with blood you couldn't tell what color it used to be. The bones were scattered across the bed, the skull set up to face the door on one of the pillows. The rest of the room was just as clean as the first scene.

"You'll want to stay out in the hall," Greg told White, before turning to me. "Vengeance?"

I knew what he was asking. The whispers came, settling on my shoulders, the figures curling through the air with us, the shadows flowing over the pockmarked wood of the floor. We looked down at the remains on the bed. They certainly looked gnawed on, and I'm no detective or coroner, but I would've guessed from the way the bones had been picked almost clean it was the same type of monster.

The figures reached out with their fingers, rolling over the skull on the pillow so that it toppled, and ended up staring up at the ceiling.

White made a noise at the door. "What did that?!"

We looked at her, and she backed up into the hallway, her face grey.

"Your eyes," Greg said.

I blinked, the whispers fading. "Did they do the black shit again?"

He shot a look at the door then came up to me so that

his breath was in my ear. "They've been doing it every time lately."

"Have you told Virgil?"

"Not yet," he admitted.

Which meant Virgil knew anyway, but I didn't tell that to Greg.

"Did they tell you anything?" he asked.

"Nothing new," I said.

He nodded and put his hand on the small of my back, steering me back over to the door. White was waiting in the hall, and while she looked somewhat strained, she led us to the second bedroom, just over and up to our left, slowly making our way back to the front of the building.

The scene was the same. This time I tilted my head to the side, eyes closed as I stood by the bed. The whispers sighed in my ears, and then the figures moved forward, clattering the bones on the bed. The noise made me open my eyes, and I turned toward the door.

"Should they sound like that?" I asked, because they had sounded hollow, and I didn't see any way for them to be hollow since they were all still whole and unbroken. Isn't bone supposed to have marrow in it?

Greg's brow was furrowed. "Have them do it again."

The figures were happy to comply. Their favorite thing to do seems to be making creepy noises because unlike the whispers, they don't have a voice.

The bones clattered together again, the hollow noise repeating.

"Is that entirely necessary?" White asked from the door.

"Checking a theory," Greg said. "Did the coroner check the bone marrow on the first victim?"

"Not that I'm aware of," White said. "Cause of death seemed obvious?"

Greg snorted and turned back to me. "Anything else to sense here?"

"I don't think so," I said, letting the whispers go.

We moved on to the third bedroom, the one overlooking the street below. And here was where we found why White told us to look out for the footprints.

In addition to all the blood on the bed, there were bloody footprints covering the wood floor, crisscrossing the room and each other. It was impossible to tell how many people had been in the room itself.

We stayed back at the door, surveying.

"It looks like there was an entire hoard of people," Greg said.

"The prints aren't right," White said. "There's only four toes on all of them. How many people only have four toes per foot?"

Greg and I both knelt to examine the prints closest to the door. She wasn't kidding; all the footprints had only four toes, for both the left and right feet. The shape of the foot was off too. It looked like it was meant to only hold four toes, rather than was simply missing the pinkie toe.

Greg's breath was in my ear again. "Did you notice how many toes the Minotaur had?"

"White, back up a lot," I said. She complied, and Greg backed up with her. They were standing back by the first bedroom before I called the whispers back.

I concentrated on the footprints. How many? I asked them.

They knew what I meant. *Five*, was what they said.

They could identify five different sets. I switched subjects, asking if they could remember what feet the Minotaur had. Here, they paused. I could feel them thinking; they had ripped him apart so quickly they hadn't taken the time to count his fingers and toes.

Not that most people would've.

We decided to try a different tact. I stood up, examining the doorframes. I didn't see anything that looked like gouging from horns, although maybe the Minotaurs would've been smart enough to turn their heads?

But five more, after we had already killed four? That could mean we had missed at least two, and they were breeding.

Or could they reproduce asexually?

No, I do not want to go down that line of thinking. I never, ever want to know how monsters make babies. I'm going to let Virgil deal with that line of thought.

Greg and White were still waiting, and I let the whispers go. I didn't want to make White any more tense than she already was.

"Vengeance?" Greg asked.

"There are five," I said.

White made a startled noise. "How can you tell?"

"My power tells me," I said, skirting around the full truth.

"Thought your power was fear."

I smirked at her. "You think I would tell Susan the full truth?"

She was silent for a moment; she looked like she was chewing it over, brow furrowed and her lips pursed. "I knew there was a reason Mason liked you." She took a moment to gather her braids back, twisting and coiling them into a bun at the back of her head. "Both of you like to fuck with people."

She wasn't entirely wrong about me.

"Are you done here?" she asked. "I think the coroner would like to get moving."

"Yes," Greg said. "Thanks for holding it for us." He put his hand back on the small of my back, steering me down the stairs and out the front door.

The cameraman had set up across the street, a not-so-prime vantage point, because a tree was directly in his shot. But maybe he had been worried about being closer to Fortress and his dark looks.

Greg scooped me up and took us into the air.

∞

When we got back to the Tower it was past three in the morning, Greg had settled me back in bed while he went to talk to Virgil. When I tried to protest, he said if I hadn't been falling asleep in the air, he would take me along.

I had grumbled and gone back to sleep. I woke up briefly when he came to bed because he had pulled me against him, doing that thing where he curls around me as much as he can.

The ringing of a phone woke us both up. Greg fumbled for it on the bedside table, set it back down and snagged mine, squinting at the screen.

He held it out to me. "It's for you."

I looked at the caller ID, groaned and answered it. "Hey, Brit."

"Oh. My. God," she said. "Are you watching the news?" How was she this loud in the morning?

"No," I said. "I never watch the news."

"Well, you might want to because in the next, hmm, five minutes, Greg's mom is going to be calling him."

Next to me Greg groaned and then heaved himself up out of bed, headed over to the living room and turned on the TV. It took him a minute to get the channel over to KBC.

Susan wasn't the one on air; it was a different anchorwoman since it was the morning news. They were talking about something to do with the stock market. I went to stand next to Greg.

"Brit, they're talking about—" I started.

"Just wait! They'll come back around to it!"

Greg and I waited, both of us impatiently standing at the back of the couch. The news did finally cycle around to the events of the other day.

"During our coverage of the latest art installation in Apollo Square, a sniper began—"

I stopped listening because the cameraman had managed to get a prime, Hollywood action shot of me at the moment I got hit. Greg's hands were on the back of the couch, and I heard the wood groan.

"Furniture," I said absently to him. He let go of the couch.

"You got shot, woman!" Brit yelled into the phone. She sounded much too excited about it.

"It's not an enjoyable experience, so I wouldn't recommend it. That shit hurts," I told her.

I could practically see the moment where she would've waved that comment off. "Wait for it," she said. "There's more."

She wasn't kidding. They had footage of the entire exterior of what was going on: the moment Greg landed, disappeared, and came back to us, the cameraman zoomed in on the remnants of the bullet from the one that had hit Greg in the face. I even got to see the moment where Ranger had gotten hit. I winced because that was not a flesh wound; that had gone straight into his shoulder, and the impact had knocked him back a couple feet.

The footage they had of the aftermath consisted of him pulling his jacket off and trying to dig the bullet out with his fingers. That apparently was the reason Greg had gone back to stay with him because there was a lot of blood oozing out past his fingers. Greg had grabbed his shoulder, pinned him against his chest and dug the bullet out for him.

The cameraman wasn't close enough to see exactly what Ranger did, but I knew what it was. Then he had snagged his jacket back off the ground and pulled it back on, completely covering his bloodied shirt.

I turned to glare at Greg. "How come no one tells me the truth about getting shot either?"

"What?" Brit said. "I would totes tell you if I got shot."

"Not you. Team member."

"Oh, that guy? He's hot. Is he single?"

"You're married."

"Tony and I have a get one free ticket rule."

"You do not!" I said, although I was giggling. Tony did

not seem like the type to be okay with that.

"Well, I have a get one free ticket rule," she said. "Hold on, they're not done. They're not even to the good part yet."

The cameraman had been smart enough not to come out from cover until after Greg had gone up and through the window of the room Mirage was in. Ranger had headed into the building from street level, and Virgil and Maniac had arrived. They cut the footage so that it looked like these things had happened almost simultaneously rather than the long minutes we spent waiting for Virgil to get there in the first place.

I was getting bored. "You know, you say there's a good part, but I'm still not seeing anything."

"Shush," she said.

They caught the moment where we had come out of the building, escorting Mirage, when he climbed into the car and Greg had loaded the bike into the back of the Hummer.

"Wait for it," Brit said.

But I had a feeling of dread in the pit of my stomach because I knew exactly which moment she was excited for.

On camera, Greg dropped to his knees, an arm wrapped around my legs as he shoved my jacket up, pressing his ear to my stomach.

I have never in my life, seen such a wide, shit-eating grin before like I did on the anchorwoman when that played out and she cheerfully announced, "It would appear Fortress and Vengeance are expecting a little bundle of joy."

In my ear, Brit squealed. I yanked the phone away from my head.

On cue, Greg's phone rang on the bedside table. He turned, strode to it and sighed, but answered it anyway. "Hey, Mom." He sighed again. "Mom, it's the news, they make things up all the—" He made an aggravated noise and went into the bathroom, shutting the door behind him.

Like I wouldn't just hang up on Brit to go listen in to his half of the conversation.

Brit was chattering now though. "Sandra and I are both so pissed!"

"You don't sound pissed," I said.

"You should've told us, like, the minute of! Now we have to plan a baby shower, and we don't even have a timeline!"

"Wait, what?"

"When are you due?" she demanded.

"Um—" I said. Dr. Hawk had come in and out so quickly that I wasn't sure it had registered.

"Oh my God, how do you not know that?" There was rustling on her end. "Doesn't matter, I'll just call Greg later, he'll remember. Steel trap, I swear. I had to call my parents to make sure they know that you'll have to do fittings up until day of to make sure the dress fits over the bump."

"What?"

"You can't honestly think after all the work Sandra and I put in that we're letting you get away with not having a wedding? Greg's mom is totally going to shit a brick. She's old fashioned."

"Really? I didn't get that vibe from her."

Brit snorted. "Right? Oh, Sandra's calling me, gotta go, we have to do damage control." She hung up on me.

I stared at the phone. Damage control for what?

My phone chose that moment to ring, and I jumped. The number on the screen was not one I was familiar with. Being stupid, I answered it. "Hello?" I said, warily.

"Are you fucking kidding me?!"

"Hi, Susan," I said. "How'd you get my number?"

"Howell got it off White's phone for me. You might want to tell her to watch her personal items around him," she said, sounding calmer.

"I'll be sure to do that. Why are you calling me?"

"When are you due?"

Oh ho ho, I am not falling for that. "When am I what?" I asked innocently.

"Do not play innocent with me," she growled. "I cannot

believe you let Hannah scoop me. Last I checked, this kind of stuff is supposed to come to me *first*."

"I am unaware of any sort of newsworthy agreement between us," I said, "and I have no idea what kind of scoop you're talking about."

But I felt absolutely smug about the fact that her own station hid this from her so they could put it on the morning news.

"Vigilante and I have an *agreement*," she was snarling at me now, "that anything like this between you and Fortress comes to me for reporting *first*."

"I'll have to ask him about that, since I wasn't informed. But I definitely did not go to another reporter with anything."

There was a pause on her end. Then, grudgingly, "I believe you didn't."

"I am curious about this agreement though," I told her. "What do you have on Vigilante that he agreed to let you be the only one we would talk to?"

There was silence on her end, the kind of embarrassed silence that could only mean one thing.

"Okay, well, if you're not going to tell me, I'm going to hang up now," I said because I needed to hightail it downstairs.

"Wait!" she said. "I want ultrasound pictures and first photos!"

"Hmm, you'll have to talk to Vigilante about that," I said, "since that's who the agreement is with." I hung up.

Greg was still in the bathroom, so the question was, which did I want to do: try to eavesdrop or head downstairs?

I could badger him about the conversation later. "I've got to go make sure Virgil knows about this!" I called in the direction of the bathroom, and then I went flying out the door barefoot.

Greg had settled me in bed still in my clothes but had taken my shoes and socks off at least.

I took the stairs two at a time, leaping down and around as I took the switchback, and then I popped out onto Virgil's floor. The laboratory door was open, so I went straight for it.

Virgil was in there, checking something in the cabinets, a clipboard on one hand. He turned to face me as I came in. "Meg, to what do I owe the pleasure?" he asked.

"When did you sleep with Susan?" I asked him.

I had managed to surprise him. I saw the flicker of it across his face before his features settled back into their usual calm, thoughtful appearance. He set the clipboard and pen down on the counter, then leaned back against it, arms crossed.

"What gave you the idea that I had?" he asked me.

"She wouldn't tell me what she's got on you to have first crack at Greg and me," I said.

"Hmm," he said. "It's because she has nothing. She did try to get something on me, but for some reason her electronics malfunctioned."

"You did not."

"I did not, that time," he admitted, "Because she had ulterior motives, and I was not going to engage in that. No matter how tempting the offer was."

"When?" I demanded.

"After the Gorgon was dead," he said. "I would stop by her place during patrols. She tends to stay up late."

"Thought you thought she was a problem."

His lips twitched, the corner of his eyes crinkling. "I do admire a person who can get one up on me."

"Is it still ongoing?"

"On occasion."

"What about Craig?"

"That is also ongoing."

"Does Susan know?"

"She knows we're not exclusive. I don't feel that telling her about Craig would be fair to him. He's never felt comfortable about publicly exposing any of his relationships, and she would report it." He paused, considering me before he spoke again. "Why do you really want to know about Susan?"

"Have you been giving information about Greg and me

to her?"

"No," Virgil said. "The agreement she is so hot and bothered about is that I would request you inform her of any developments that she would be interested in. I did not tell her at what time I would place the request."

"Was it never?"

Virgil's eyes were dancing. "It may have been."

"Yet you still slept with her," I pointed out.

"The supposed agreement came well after that point," he said. "If information on the two of you had been her only motive, I never would have. I compromise many things; I will not compromise that." He must have sensed that I was about to argue again. "Meg, I can quite clearly sense whether consent is full and willing. I am not going to engage if it's anything but. What is it you say? I'm not into that?"

"Does Greg know?" I asked him.

"He's known since she first approached me."

"How much shit are you two hiding from me?"

His lips twitched again. "About as much shit as you and I are hiding from Greg."

I opened my mouth, closed it, and thought about it. "Are Ranger and Maniac the only ones on this team without any secrets?"

"I believe Ranger is keeping secrets only from himself," Virgil said. "Maniac is an open book."

The door in the hallway opened and closed. I heard the padding of bare feet, and then Greg poked his head around the door. "Am I allowed in on this party line?"

Virgil waved a hand at the room. "Take a seat. I believe Meg had something she needed to inform me of."

"Susan wants ultrasound and first photos," I said.

"No," Greg said. "I'm not letting her use our baby as fodder for the masses."

"You don't believe she'll try and get footage of the three of you any time you're out?"

"It's not like we'll be taking a baby on missions with us,"

Greg said pointedly.

Virgil snorted. "As if you won't have to take him with you any other time? He'll have doctor's appointments at the very least. What about when you just want to go out together? Visits to the park once he's old enough?"

Greg was grinding his teeth. "I'm not – he's not a prop. This isn't just footage of us. We're adults, we can make that decision for ourselves."

"I think you'll want to get out ahead of this to protect his privacy," Virgil said. "It's not often two heroes have a child together. People are going to be curious."

Greg scrubbed at his face, pushed his hair back. "God damn it." He was thinking, his brow furrowed. "What do you want to do?"

Both of them were looking at me. "Who, me?" I asked.

"Yes, you," Greg said, sounding amused. "He's your baby too. What do you want to do about Susan?"

I thought about it. "Susan can have exclusive photos about any important events, but no ultrasound photos *and* she has to work to get her station to squash any other information. Like trips to the park."

Greg's lips twitched. "What counts as important events?"

"None of them."

"I feel like there are some that would qualify," he said.

"Depends on your point of view."

He was grinning at me. "You're going to completely ignore his first birthday as an event?"

"He won't remember it."

"I'll handle Susan, and her – expectations," Virgil said. "In the meantime, Greg, I will need you, Maniac and Ranger to go check the subway tunnels again. We're going to go section by section for process of elimination."

"What about me?"

"I'm requesting that you stay here until I have a new suit for you," Virgil said.

"What, with Mirage?"

"No, with me," Virgil said. "I would not leave you alone in the same building as him."

"Which apartment did you put him in, and what are we doing about him?" Greg asked.

"I've put out some feelers on anyone that would've put out a hit on a dead person," Virgil said. "Now, if you could please go collect Ranger and Maniac and head out. When I have any results on the Mirage front, I will inform you."

CHAPTER SEVEN

Greg headed down while I headed up. A few minutes later, he came back to our apartment. I had poured myself a bowl of cereal and was sitting at the island eating and waiting on the coffee to brew when he came in.

"You locked the balcony door," he said, sounding pleased.

"You said any time you weren't in the apartment with me."

He hit the button in the controls on the wall so the door would unlock, then came over and gave me a kiss. "I'll call you when we're done. My mom wants us to come have dinner."

"Do we have to?" I asked.

"Yes, we have to. She wants to go out for a change."

"Hmm," I said. "She's up to something."

"Probably," he said cheerfully. He kissed me again, his hand in my hair. When he pulled back, he left his hand there. "Watch yourself."

"Always. I'm not the one going out to fight Minotaurs, though."

He chuckled and headed out the balcony door. When he took off, I got up and relocked the door.

Now I was locked in the Tower.

Being stuck inside when you're not the one to choose it

gets boring very quickly. Well, Virgil and Greg hadn't said I wasn't allowed to leave, just that I wasn't going on missions. And we all know how well I would listen if they had tried to order me not to leave at all. But my only choices for places to go were the coffee shop up the street or to any of the number of restaurants nearby.

I suppose I could have gotten on the bus to go get groceries, but we were stocked up.

I needed to replace the shirt that Greg tore yesterday, but for that I just go to Goodwill or a consignment store, and like groceries, that would also require a bus trip.

What I ended up doing was taking a shower and then cleaning up around the apartment. There wasn't much to do, and the most onerous thing was going to be the laundry. Not because it's hard, just because of folding and putting things away.

Oh yeah, Virgil put washers and dryers in the apartments. Ours is in a little closet in the bathroom. He didn't want us having to waste time waiting on things at laundromats.

Once I had the clothes in the washer, I headed over to the fridge. At barely 10 am technically it wasn't late enough to be drinking soda, but I ignore that rule whenever I feel like it.

It's a self-imposed rule. Greg has never said a word about what time of day I choose to switch from coffee to soda.

I opened the fridge, and I realized he had switched out my regular sodas for root beer. I'm not complaining about the type of soda; I'm just trying to figure out when he did that because the fridge pack that had been in there had still been mostly full, so he hadn't just replaced an empty or almost empty box.

He had already popped the piece of perforated cardboard off of it too, one soda sitting on the shelf. I was reaching to grab the can when a god appeared in the kitchen.

There had been nothing there, and then I could feel his presence looming at my back. The hair on the back of my neck stood up, and the muscles in my shoulders tensed, my heart hammering in my chest. Slowly, I straightened up, shut the fridge door, and then tried to dart to my right, but his arm was in my way, the palm of his hand set on the cabinet door. When I tried to turn and go the other way, I found I was trapped, his left arm and body blocking the way, and now my back was against the fridge itself. He moved in closer to me, and I shrunk as much as I could, face averted, eyes on the floor.

I had seen enough to see his anchor looked much the same as the impression I had gotten in that cylindrical prison I went to when I temporarily died, although his dark hair had been cut short so that the curl to it gave more the impression of waves. He was wearing a suit, the grey sleeve of it still in my view.

He had chuckled when I had bumped back into the fridge, the timbre of his voice still deep and filled with thunder. A curiously calm part of my mind recalled Ares' voice, how harsh it always was, and filed away the fact that maybe the anchors' voices went to sleep with them when the gods took them over.

The whispers were at my back, figures curling and swirling around me, the shadows rising up, even as they cowered back from his power. Cautious and quiet they were, and it made my breath come in panicked gasps because it felt like they were preparing for whatever was about to come. I had to calm down or I would hyperventilate, and I didn't know if the Furies would fight back against him or if I would be left without any form of protection.

His lips were hovering over my shoulder, his face sliding past my neck, his breath tickling the skin and ruffling the curls. His voice was in my ear, menacing in its seductiveness.

"I don't remember you preferring such anchors. You were always so – sharp – in appearance."

I squeaked and tried to slide away, but it just brought me closer to the arm in my way, and now the space I had from him was even smaller, the cage of his body closing tighter around me. If I could have climbed into the fridge to get away from him in that moment, I would've.

His lips were hovering over my shoulder again, and he took a deep shuddering breath that made my stomach turn.

Then he paused, the cage around me suddenly opening as he stepped back from me. "You have Hera's blessing," he said, sounding both angry and suspicious.

I tried to sidle away, but he blocked me again. I kept my eyes down. The whispers and I were unsure if he wanted an answer, and we didn't want him angry at us.

He leaned back in over me, his voice in my ear again, commanding. "Refute it."

Oh fuck. Now I was going to have no choice; I had to say something. My mouth dry, my arms folded over my stomach, I made myself as small, as subservient in appearance as I could.

"I can't," I whispered. Let him be mad at Hera and not at me. Let him think I had no choice in this and that I wasn't refusing him, at least until I could get away from him. Was there anywhere he wouldn't find us?

He backed away again, and although his face was dark, it was also considering. I heard the lock on the front door as it flipped, the hinges creak as it swung open. The whispers vanished.

"Meg?" Virgil's voice, and my knees almost gave out in relief. He would step carefully around this god.

"In the kitchen," I called out, my voice cracking. "I have a visitor."

"I am aware," Virgil said dryly, having stopped as he came around, taking in the tableau. "I didn't want to interrupt, but we have an urgent development."

Zeus stepped farther away from me. "So, you are collecting mortals."

"Personal project," I said, the words popping out of my mouth before I thought them through. I swore inwardly. Don't sass the god!

But he chuckled, amused. "We will speak later." Then

he vanished.

Virgil and I both stayed still, frozen for several more heartbeats while we waited, tense and expectant. I was terrified he would return.

My legs finally gave out, and Virgil rushed forward to catch me. I was shaking.

"Which one was it?" Virgil said, visibly alarmed.

"Zeus," I gasped out.

"Fuck," he said.

It was at this point that I giggled.

"No. Do not have hysterics. Breathe." I could hear the command in his voice, floating in the air.

I took a breath. Then another. "Thought you didn't use that on anyone on the team," I said when I had calmed down.

"I don't use it on anyone on the team. This is a special case. What happened?"

"He just showed up behind me in the kitchen."

"Did he do anything? Are you hurt? Is the baby hurt? Are they hurt?"

"He had me trapped against the fridge, but no, he didn't touch me. We're fine, all of us."

Virgil waited, watching me silently.

"He told me to refute Hera's blessing. I told him I couldn't."

"Okay, up on your feet. You're coming down to my apartment."

Virgil helped me up and towed me out the door and down the stairs. He got me settled on the couch in his apartment, then disappeared back out his front door. When he came back, he went through the living room into his kitchen, came out, and set a root beer down on the coffee table in front of me.

I stared at it. "What is this?"

"It's a soda," he said.

"I can see that. You don't drink soda."

"I'm stocking these specifically for you."

"Why are you and Greg both stocking root beer?"

"They don't have caffeine."

Oh. The whole "watch the caffeine" rule. Now that I thought about it, the amount of coffee in the pot had been mysteriously low recently. "Thanks," I said, picking the soda up and popping it open.

"You're welcome." Virgil moved away, sitting down in one of the armchairs, settling one ankle across one knee, his fingers steepled as he watched me.

He was doing it on purpose because the silence was stretching. "Did you hear anything back about Mirage?" I asked.

"Not yet. I expect it will be a couple days before anyone ferrets anything out for me."

"Where is Mirage?"

"I locked him into a panic room on the floor below Ranger's."

I snickered. "How'd you convince him to go into one?"

"It's a panic room."

"You used the thing on him, didn't you?"

"I may have – helped – his decision along," Virgil admitted. He pulled out his phone, scrolled and then texted a message. "I do need to inform Greg that you are sitting with me, and not to worry when he finds your balcony door unlocked."

"Are we going to tell him?"

"About Zeus?" Virgil steepled his fingers again, his brow furrowed. "I do – worry – about his ability to function if his attention is constantly divided by what could be happening to you. I do not know how else to explain my recommendation to him that you move, at least temporarily, to the empty apartment on this floor."

"Won't they just find me there?"

"There is that possibility," Virgil admitted. "I'm hoping that having mine or another's presence around you will be something of a deterrent. So far, the others have only appeared when you're alone, correct?"

"Not Bacchu—" I started, but the first time he had shown up I had been on my own, even though it was only for those few minutes. Ares had approached me in public, and while there were other people around me, it wasn't anyone I knew. And I think that time he kind of stumbled across me. I sighed. "Okay, so Bacchus will approach me when I'm around other people, but so far, the really powerful ones, no."

Why is that? Why do they always wait until I'm on my own? Other than the once, even Ares won't come find me when I'm around people; he makes me come to him. Any time they've shown up with the others present, it's always been in a way where I've had to go to them as well.

Virgil nodded, looking thoughtful, then he got up and disappeared from the living room again. When he came back, he was carrying a stack of books, and he set them down on the coffee table before he sat back down in his armchair, snagging the top book up as he went. He crossed his ankle over his knee again, settling the book against his leg as he flipped it open and started to read.

"Are you researching again?" I asked.

"Hmm, no, this is for fun."

I studied the pile of books. They were all about gardening. I tried to peek over at the page he was reading, but the angle was wrong; I would have to get up and lean over him to see what that one was about. "Where are you going to put a garden?"

"We could build beds for the roof," he said, "and the railing of the balcony could hold some boxes."

"You don't seem like the gardening type," I said, thinking back to the overgrown state of the compound.

"A garden requires tending. Tending requires care. Care shows that someone lives there."

"You don't think someone would get that impression from having a garden on the roof?"

He still didn't look up from the book. "Yes, but as we

are mid-downtown, I doubt it will draw the kind of attention I would like to avoid."

"Villain attention?"

"Government, villain, reporter. Take your pick." His phone pinged and he pulled it out. "Greg says okay."

"That's it?"

"Yes."

After that, the conversation petered out, and I ended up reading about gardening from another of Virgil's books.

∞

When Greg had gotten back, he came straight down to Virgil's apartment, and he stopped in the living room door, staring at us, one hand braced on the doorframe.

"What happened?" he asked.

"What makes you think something happened?" Virgil asked calmly, still focused on the page in front of him. He flipped it over, his eyes traveling down the next page.

Greg made an irritated noise. "You both immediately tensed when I came in. Something happened."

Virgil closed his book, set it down on the coffee table, and leaned back in his chair, fingers steepled again. "I would like for Ranger and Maniac to be here before we discuss it." He waved a hand at the couch. "Come sit."

"Meg," Greg said. I looked up at him, and when we locked eyes, I heard the wood under his fingers snap. Hastily, he pulled his hand away, but it was too late, there was already a hand shaped, well, it was more than an impression since it was too deep in the wood for that, so a hand shaped hole in the frame. "Damn it," he said, but he didn't move from the doorway. "Do you owe anyone anything this time?"

"No," I said.

He nodded, took a breath, and came and sat on the couch as I scooted down so he could sit by the arm. He settled next to me, his arm across my shoulders, the other resting on the arm of the couch. He turned his head so his nose was in my hair.

"Did you locate any other Minotaurs?" Virgil asked.

"No. We're going to want to check the sewers again. Both systems this time, I think."

Virgil sighed. "I'll want to acquire some separate suiting for all of us for the sewage system. I don't think we want to be breathing that in."

Greg tilted his head to the side, considering. "They were pretty delicate, for monsters. Do you think they could even live in there?"

Virgil put a hand up to his chin. "I don't know if we should risk that assumption."

Boots in the hallway. Greg must have left the front door open. Ranger and Maniac came through the door; they also paused just inside the room.

Virgil waved at the couches again. "Sit."

Ranger went and chose one of the armchairs; Maniac stayed back by the door. "Why does this look like we're about to have an intervention?" she asked.

"You attend a lot of those?" Greg asked.

She rolled her eyes but came to sit down on the couch across from us. "Yeah, as the interventee. Is that a word? Whatever, doesn't matter. My aunts kept bringing in the pastor to give me lectures about the path I was on."

"Guess they didn't stick."

"When people tell you that you're going to Hell regardless, it doesn't really work."

"That does sound like it would have the opposite effect of what's intended," Greg said, sounding thoughtful.

"Doubt the golden boy would know what it's like."

Greg's fingers flexed against me, but not in the way they do when he's mad. "You might find I understand more than you think."

She snorted. "Yeah, like you ever did anything bad in your life."

"Greg used to steal cars," I said.

That surprised her. "You did not," she said.

"I did."

Ranger leaned forward. "Wait, wait, attack dog isn't sin free?"

"Are any of us?" Greg asked.

"What else did you do?" Ranger asked, choosing to skip past the question.

"He wrecked them," I said, "but he won't tell me the number."

Ranger grinned at us. "If Greg was stealing cars, what kind of shit did you get up to, Meg?"

"I didn't," I said. At the strain in my voice, Greg's arm tightened, and Ranger had heard it too because his face turned serious. Even Maniac was watching me.

"Do you want me to explain it?" she asked.

"What do you know about it?" I asked her.

She shrugged. "The villains talk. Grenadier told me what he knew from Flayer."

"You did a lot of talking with Grenadier," Ranger said.

"We're going to have this conversation now?" Maniac asked. "You going to ask me about my number?"

Ranger snorted. "No. Don't need to know, just curious about the talking to begin with."

"This is entirely off topic," Virgil said.

Ranger waved a hand at him. "I don't think it is. I think we should all know about each other. Team spirit."

"You going to teach us a chant?" Greg asked.

"I'm not the one who looks like they would've been on the cheerleading squad."

"Thought I was a muscle head."

"I meant Meg. She looks like they would've been able to toss her around."

"I did track," I said.

"That doesn't sound like it would be conducive to hijinks," Ranger said.

"Meg murdered an entire group of her classmates," Maniac said. At the stunned silence, she looked around at us. "What? Band-aid. Come on, people."

"You what?" Ranger said weakly.

"Someone had drugged her," Greg said quietly.

"Someone gave me the drugs and I took them," I corrected. The guilt won't let me do anything but take responsibility for it.

"Yeah? Because the forensics team they had in there found evidence your drink had been roofied," Greg said.

I twisted to look at him. "What? What team? How did they even know which one was mine? Why didn't you mention this to me before?" I could hear my volume rising, my voice cracking, but I couldn't help it.

"I wasn't sure which drugs had the effect on you until after Bolt tried to sedate you."

"And you didn't think to tell me sooner?" I was angry at this point, but his arm was still across my shoulder, and I couldn't move away from him.

"Meg," he said, "you were still healing, and we had to run at that point, and then – it just seemed like telling you at any point after that wouldn't help."

"What were the ones I took?" I was still trying to process the fact that no one had thought to tell me, at any point, the actual sequence events. That there had been drugs in play I was completely unaware of.

"Adderall, uppers. Between those, the ones in your drink, and the alcohol, you were lucky you didn't die."

No wonder the Furies had been so full of rage, and they wouldn't have known who to direct all of it at because I hadn't paid attention to who had given me anything.

The knowledge didn't feel like it absolved me of anything, though.

I switched targets. "Is this some of the shit the two of you are hiding from me?" I snapped at Virgil.

"Yes," he said.

Maniac leaned back against the couch cushions. "You know, if we're family, maybe we shouldn't be keeping secrets."

Virgil had a hand up at his chin. "Perhaps. Which brings us to why I called this meeting." He waited for us to all turn our attention to him. "Meg had a visitor while you were all gone."

"Which one?" Ranger asked.

"Zeus," Virgil said.

"What?" Greg said, and I heard his voice crack, felt his arm tighten against me again. "Are you both okay?"

"We're fine," I said, soothing. "He didn't touch me."

"I believe you, but can I check?"

"You ask now?" I said, teasing, "but not in the street?"

He cleared his throat, looking sheepish, "I might have reacted before I thought it through."

"You can check any time you need to."

He smiled at that, moving off the couch to kneel beside me and press his ear to my stomach, his chin in my lap again.

"You two are sickeningly adorable," Maniac said.

Greg's fingers flexed against my legs; his eyes closed. "He's fine."

"Which brings us to why Zeus didn't cause any harm to Meg," Virgil said.

Greg stayed on the floor, looking between us. "Why?"

"It would appear that Hera has bestowed some level of – protection – on Meg," Virgil said.

"When?" Greg asked.

Virgil focused on me. "Would you like to tell him?"

"Band-aid," Maniac said. "You guys seriously need to learn to just spit this shit out."

"Camping trip," I said.

"*When?*" Greg repeated.

"Lake shore. Right before you came out of the tent."

He got up and stepped back from me. "What did she do?"

"She gave me her blessing—" I started.

"What does that mean?" he interrupted. "What does –" his eyes widened. "Did she – she didn't—" he sounded horrified.

"No. No compulsions," I said. I was positive she hadn't done anything to him; when I thought back to it, I was the only one she had touched, the only one she might have compelled.

He heard the truth of it in my voice, in the beat of my heart, and he took a breath. "Okay, okay." Then his eyes narrowed. "Is she the reason your IUD is gone?"

"I'm pretty sure she is."

He had a hand in his hair. "This is our child, right? She didn't just, make him appear?"

I had to pause for a moment to figure out how to answer him, so I didn't end up answering the wrong question with a positive.

"Meg," he said, pleading.

"He's ours," I said. "Her power is related to fertility, not immaculate conception." Related as in childbirth itself. I didn't remember the tales talking about her being a fertility goddess specifically, but we all know where the tales had gotten us so far.

He sat down too hard on the coffee table, the whole thing collapsing beneath him. "God damn it," he swore, but he sounded too relieved to be mad at himself for the unintentional furniture destruction.

"So, what happened?' Ranger asked.

"From what Meg tells me, Zeus showed up in the kitchen, and when he realized Hera had protected her, he ordered her to refute it. Whether that means refuse Hera's 'help' or the side effect of it was unclear. Obviously, Meg did no such thing."

Greg was looking at Virgil from the remnants of the table. "What part aren't you telling us?"

"He did say he would be back to talk to her."

"What—" Greg's voice cracked again, so he cleared his

throat. "What can we do to prevent that?"

Maniac had crossed her arms and legs and was watching us. "Why are they all so interested in Meg?"

That made all of us pause. Why *were* they harassing me? Even the hero recruitment hadn't been this intense.

Virgil was steepling his fingers. "A good question. There must be something about the Furies that they are drawn to. Or they want their skills for something."

"Well, I think we can set at least one of them very firmly in one 'why' category," I said. "Because he seemed very focused on his creepy 'seduction' technique."

Greg made that strangled sound.

"He would lose interest after a while," I said.

"That is not helping," he said. "I can't – we can't – just let him do that to you because he'll lose interest later!"

"You have got to work on your people skills," Maniac said. "Was that supposed to be reassuring? Because I don't think any of us are reassured."

I looked at the floor. "I'm trying to be a realist. Even Hera wasn't safe from him. He straight up tricked her and then trapped her in marriage." Even historians had Zeus listed as one of the first known villains; after a lot of heated debate, he had been stripped of his hero-status regardless of what the tales said.

"It would, however, appear – at least for now – that Zeus is not going to risk Hera's anger while her blessing is in effect," Virgil inserted before anyone could start panicking, "and most of these gods have not approached Meg when others known to her are present. So, Meg, who gets first shift?"

"First what?" I said at the same time that Greg said, "I do."

"You do what?" I demanded.

"I'm taking first shift."

"For what?"

"At this time, I believe it would be prudent of everyone to take shifts staying with you at all times to discourage the gods from popping in at all," Virgil said. "Greg, I would also recommend you retrieve anything you need immediate use of from your apartment and both of you temporarily relocate to this floor. I want to circle the wagons, so to say, so Meg's got backup steps away rather than a floor or two."

Greg heaved himself off the floor and headed out of the apartment.

"You don't think this is going to hamper us in terms of missions?" I asked. "We have Minotaurs out there eating people."

"We are going to end up spread thin, or you will have to accompany us as part of the teams before you're re-outfitted."

Ranger leaned forward again. "Should we be asking for help? I know a lot of other heroes are in bed with the government, but this is turning into something big."

Virgil didn't move from his position, but his brow furrowed. "I hate to admit it, but this is becoming much larger than a five-person team can handle."

"It's maneaters," I said. "What could we possibly need help with that for?"

"Do you just wear blinders for everything?" Maniac asked. "You have literal gods stalking you. We need a squadron or something."

"And what's the price for the others to come in and help us?" I asked. "Are we all going to end up contracted for life?"

"A leap from the frying pan into the fire," Virgil muttered. "Unlike most of you, I was around when France happened."

Ranger looked up from his hands. "Seriously? How old are you anyway?"

"Fifty-four," Virgil said.

"You don't look fifty-four." Maniac said.

"Good genes," Virgil said, "but it does mean I have double the life experience of a couple of you, so I hope you'll seriously consider my advice when I tell you, do not trust the government to have our best interests at heart."

"You don't need to tell me twice," Maniac said.

Greg came back in, our shared suitcase tucked under one arm. "Tell you twice about what?"

"Don't trust the government," Maniac said.

Greg snorted. "Yeah, don't."

Ranger smirked. "What kind of conspiracy theorists did I just lump myself in with?"

Greg inclined his head. "Virgil started it. He warned me. He said they would piss me off eventually, and that hopefully it would be something small and not catastrophic."

"Didn't realize you were military," Ranger said.

"Once upon a time," Greg said. "Back before I realized what they considered acceptable."

Maniac snorted. "Why did it take you so long? The others knew from the start."

"They knew what I could do," Greg said. "They were careful about who they had handling and giving me orders so I wouldn't hear the lie."

"Was it Bolt?" I asked.

Greg set the suitcase down. "Yes," he said. "I didn't know she could control her heartbeat."

"Was she the one who said it was acceptable if I died?" I asked, incredulous that he would trust her at all after that.

"No," he said. "If she had, well, maybe things would've turned out differently." He sighed and spoke before I could say anything. "Not like that Meg. I never would've risked anyone, like that. Especially not you. But I might have told you the truth about Red Eye sooner."

"You hid shit from Meg from the start?" Ranger said. "You're still hiding shit from her?"

Greg was silent, standing by our suitcase.

"You—" Ranger started. "How is that healthy?" he demanded. "You two are married, you're having a kid! Talk to each other for Christ's sake!" He shoved himself up from his chair and pointed at me. "For the record, I don't pull this bullshit on you." And he stormed out.

Maniac sighed. "Some therapy session this was."
"I thought it was an intervention," I said.
"Same difference," she said.

CHAPTER EIGHT

Virgil ended up sending Maniac down to talk to Ranger and told both Greg and me he was just going to air all the dirty laundry because Ranger and Maniac were right: all of us needed to stop hiding things from each other.

We've got enough shit going on. We don't need to start causing divisions because we won't just talk to each other.

Virgil made Greg and me sit back down next to each other on the couch and then sat across from us.

"We're going to start with you, Meg," Virgil said.

"Wait, why do I have to go first? You already spilled my beans."

Virgil waved my comment off. "No, we're going to start with you in terms of the things that affect you. So, Greg did not tell you about the drugs at my request."

"Why?"

"I may have gotten a copy of your file."

"May have?" I said suspiciously.

"I did get a copy of your file."

"Where is it?"

"Destroyed, after I read it."

I crossed my arms. "Then what's my favorite color?" Next to me, Greg snorted.

"That line was left curiously blank," Virgil said. "Greg

was willing to go along with my request because, as he said, he did not feel the knowledge would help you at the time." He paused. "I didn't feel it would be helpful for you either. Your reaction to sedatives is extreme."

"We left right after Bolt. It couldn't have been that—"

"No, we didn't," Virgil said. "You were out of it for three days. The only reason Greg wasn't in more of a panic over you being that way was because we could at least rouse you enough to answer us."

I thought back. "I don't remember any—"

"No, you don't. I don't know that you ever will," Virgil said. "It took Greg a full day to rouse you and get you off the floor to start with."

"But you – you asked what happened. I heard that!"

"Hmm, yes, because whatever happened when Bolt tried to tranq you knocked me on my ass. Greg found me on the floor of the lab, and I couldn't get near my room. He could. And then he wouldn't answer me until after he had made sure you were taken care of."

I was thinking. "Where were you two? Bolt tried to take me down to the garage."

"The lab has another secret entrance, down to a second security room where I keep all the tapes from what my bugs record. Greg and I had gone down there, and almost as soon as he was there, I knew something was wrong."

"He went flying back up the stairs without telling me what was going on," Greg said. "When I got up there, he was already down, and I couldn't get past the lab door at first. By the time I got down to his room, he couldn't get down the hallway."

"The effect lingered for over an hour after Greg had finally gotten to you," Virgil said. "It was after that I got a copy of your file."

"From whom?" I asked.

"Striker. He overloaded the locks for the records room and sent me scans."

"He keeps doing things for you two."

"He does," Virgil said mildly. "We'll have to offer him a spot when his contract comes up in April. We'll need the coverage."

Greg scrubbed at his face. "Can we just get to the point?"

"Hmm, yes. Now, initially I thought that it was just a bad interaction, something to do with the drugs strengthening or exacerbating the effects of your power. But now, with gods showing up every which way we turn, I'm wondering if what it's really doing is freeing the Furies from whatever happened when they chose to anchor themselves the way they did."

"You want to test this?" I asked cautiously.

"No," Virgil said. "Even if it weren't for your pregnancy, I would not feel comfortable subjecting you to the kind of testing we would have to do. I think we can safely theorize that the sedatives have that effect, but dosing you with Adderall or alcohol just to see if it would have a similar effect? Absolutely not. We have no way of knowing what would happen overall."

"Okay," I said, relieved.

I would have refused if Virgil had wanted to test it, but if he had been open to that kind of testing in the first place, it would have made me nervous.

"I told you she was underutilizing them," Greg said.

"So you did," Virgil said. "I don't think either of us realized it was to this extent."

"I'm not underutilizing them—" I protested.

"Yes, you are," Greg said. "You're doing more, but the power you were putting out when Bolt knocked you out – that shows they're still not using their full strength."

"If Red Eye had sedated you in the hospital, he would've died in that moment," Virgil said. "The Furies have hampered themselves, and the question is why. Did they intend to, or was it an accident?"

"Why didn't you just drug me and then trap him?" Now

I was angry they would risk themselves when they had a guaranteed outcome.

"Meg, how do you know they wouldn't have come after us, too?" Greg said.

"I did leave the information in the compound for you for if you had to run," Virgil said quietly. "Then you would have been at a safe house, with no other people around at risk. You did not do as I expected."

"You could've just drugged and left me there," I said.

"Could we have?" Virgil asked.

I opened my mouth to argue before I realized Greg wouldn't have stood for it. Virgil could tell him that Red Eye would have died until he was blue in the face, and Greg still wouldn't have risked me. Instead, I crossed my arms, refusing to look either of them in the eyes. "You're both idiots."

"For what it's worth, we felt it was better left as a measure of last resort. And Mirage was supposed to cover you as well so you could get out," Virgil said. "Coward."

"He did try to make me run before he took off into the door," I admitted.

Greg shoved his hair back. "You would refuse to."

"So, what now?" I asked. "What does any of this mean?"

"How many of the gods realize you're not what you should be, anchoring and power strength-wise?" Virgil asked.

"Ares, Bacchus, and Poseidon all know something is wrong," I said. "I don't know if they know the extent."

Virgil waved it off. "I know about Ares. Is he the only one who knows about how you're anchored?"

"As far as I know," I said. "Poseidon called me 'fragile?' Bacchus just seems to know something isn't right about it."

"What about Hera? Did Zeus say anything when he was with you?"

"No. Neither of them seemed to notice anything."

Virgil's hand was up at his chin. "So all we can conclude is that your anchoring is different, and other than the fact that the Furies anchored themselves before you were born, we don't know what's important about that distinction. Is it the timing that affected the change or something else? How are the other gods anchored?"

"I don't know," I said. I don't think Virgil was expecting a different answer though.

"Back to our earlier topic. Would Ares be able to tell us why the interest?"

"I don't know, and the question is whether he would even be willing to. It could be that they're all running their own projects and I fit into them. The gopher god."

Virgil pinched his nose. "I hate to leave a source of information untouched, but we risk indebting Meg, or even ourselves, to them for answers."

"Ares did give us information without requiring anything from us when it came to the Gorgon." Greg said.

"No, he gave *me* information because of the history he and the Furies have," I said. "I don't think we can attribute his altruism to anything else, and we can't depend on it to give us answers."

He hadn't given us a direct answer about the Gorgon and the Hydras to start with anyway.

Greg grunted. "I was hoping for an easy one for a change."

"Makes you long for the days where it was just drugs, doesn't it?" Virgil said.

I was thinking. "You let Bolt's remains sit for three days?"

"Two, technically, since for the first one we couldn't get in there anyway," Virgil said, "and yes, we did, because we were busy trying to rouse you and couldn't risk moving things outside when we didn't know how long we had or if Red Eye was going to show back up."

No wonder the room had smelled so bad. I'm surprised Virgil got the stench out at all.

"How much of this have you told Ranger?" I asked.

"Only about Red Eye and his attempts to murder you. He's missing most of the story."

"Are you and Greg hiding anything else from me?"

"Eleven," Greg said.

"Eleven what?" I asked, confused by the subject change.

"I wrecked eleven of them."

"You stole eleven cars to start with?"

"No, I think I was there for closer to fifty or so of them."

"What the hell were you doing?" I asked.

Greg cleared his throat and looked at the floor. "I was working for a chop shop."

"And they were okay with you wrecking eleven cars?"

"I only got paid for the ones I brought in."

Virgil clapped his hands together. "Well, I feel better. Let's go tell Ranger the happy news."

"Excuse me," I said, "but don't you have a confession to make?"

"Oh, yes, that. Greg, I'm psychic, so very rarely can you hide things from me. Oh, and I can influence people to do things. I don't use this on anyone on the team. But my timing, that's just very good timing."

"Yeah, was the paintball gun necessary?" I asked.

"No," Virgil said, his lips twitching, "but the bruises would've been worse."

∞

Virgil dragged the two of us down to Ranger's apartment. I say Ranger's because even though he and Maniac are essentially living together, she still has one set aside for her across the hall.

I haven't been inside it yet. Come to think of it, I never went inside his apartment back in our temporary headquarters either.

Virgil knocked on the door, and Ranger answered it. He

had taken off his jacket at some point, so when he opened the door and leaned against the frame, blocking the way in, I could see that the jacket itself didn't add much heft across his shoulders.

He didn't have the same mass that Greg had, though, his frame was smaller.

Except for when the news caught him without it, and that one night in the compound, I had rarely seen him without his jacket. At the nighttime encounter, I had initially been too embarrassed to really give him any sort of look over other than to notice the scars the figures had left up his arm and across his ribs.

"What?" he said.

"May we come in?" Virgil asked.

"I don't know. Are we going to keep hiding shit from each other?"

"No, I feel it's time we discuss what's going on and explain things in detail."

Ranger stepped back, opening the door the rest of the way, and motioned us inside.

His apartment was very bare.

He had opted for the studio version too. The living room contained a two-seater couch, a coffee table, and a small table on which rested a TV, not even a real entertainment center. There was nothing in the dining room area, some stools under the kitchen counter, and then the bed over on the other end of the room.

No wonder Maniac kept her own apartment.

Look, I didn't have much furniture when I was on my own either; I'm super spoiled now. But my apartment still looked lived in.

Virgil looked at the room, then looked at Ranger. "Where's the rest of it?"

"Next door."

"You took the furniture out?" Greg asked.

"It made everything crowded." Ranger motioned at the

room. "You can sit somewhere. Pull out a stool. I don't do a whole lot of entertaining."

"You don't say," I said.

Ranger's lips twitched. "I used to just go back to their place."

Well, I wasn't going wherever he was trying to take that conversation. "Those dinner parties must have been extra awkward." Damn it, I still did, didn't I?

He grinned at me.

Greg cleared his throat. "I think, technically, we're here to admit you're right."

"Don't tell me, tell Meg," Ranger said.

"We already did," Virgil said, "and in the interest of full disclosure, we will need Maniac here as well."

Ranger went past us, back to the front door, and to the one across the hall. He knocked and yelled. "Yo, Maniac, they're here to tell us we're right."

I heard the door open and close, and then Maniac and Ranger had come into Ranger's apartment.

"Are you going to just spit it out, or are you going to make Ranger and me drag it out of you question by question?" she asked. "Because some of us don't have time for that."

Virgil ended up being the one to tell the story. When he had initially told it to Ranger, he glossed over most of the details and had left it to Ranger to assume Red Eye had a similar immunity to what I could do as he himself had and that it was simply bad luck that I had gotten picked as one of his targets.

He had not told Ranger that Red Eye was stealing powers, or that he had done it to at least eight villains before he had come across me, and that at some point, he had started following me through my dreams, causing nightmares whenever he was nearby.

He had also failed to mention that while Greg had come to my aid, he hadn't told me what Red Eye was capable of, and that when I had found out, my reaction had been severe.

And while he had told him that Red Eye had managed to

capture and torture me, he had left out the part where it took them four weeks to get me to wake back up. And Bolt had been left out of the picture altogether.

As had Mirage. Virgil had managed to make it sound like the trap had simply been a lucky break, and the reason for Red Eye's death had been related to my reaction then being similar to when I had found out the truth, overriding whatever immunity he had. To Ranger, it had been believable, since the figures and shadows could still touch him, even if the fear the whispers put out couldn't.

He made sure to go ahead and inform both Ranger and Maniac of the part where Bolt had drugged me and the resulting three days.

When he was done, Ranger stared at us. "Four weeks?" he said.

"And then another three days," Greg said.

"Jesus." Ranger was half sitting, half leaning on the arm of his couch, one hand up at the back of his own neck. "That's not – that's not normal."

"We know," Virgil said dryly.

"Where did he disappear to for four weeks?" Maniac asked.

"We've never been able to determine that," Virgil said. "I've had contacts continue to scour for any villains or heroes who may have disappeared in that time frame, but they haven't come up with anything. Not even for any of the small powers, the ones who stay hidden as a rule."

"And he's really dead?" Ranger asked. "Because we have a problem with those."

"Yes," I said. "They tore him, and his power, apart."

"Vengeance, huh?"

"All that and more."

"So, Mirage is pissed because he thought you guys exposed him after you blackmailed him into helping in the first place?"

"Yup. And it's his own fault his nose got broken."

"What were Red Eye's plans if he had gotten Meg's power? Or, well, pulled the Furies out of her. Would that even have worked?" Maniac asked.

"Unknown, and unknown. From what Meg told me, it appeared to be working," Virgil said.

"Which," Ranger started, but paused when he looked at me. "If – don't give me that look, Meg – if she was in as bad of shape as you're saying, how did you –" he stopped again, looking frustrated.

"My power is greater than I tend to let on," Virgil admitted. "Holding a human body together so it can heal is taxing to say the least."

"Stitches," Maniac said.

"I was unsure of how Meg would react to anesthetics, and she would've needed them for me to perform that kind of procedure. Use of my power was safer for her. Greg had already warned me not to use drugs on her since he had read her file. We were unaware which one, or if it was the combination of the three, that had proved fatal for her classmates."

"Jesus," Ranger repeated.

"I don't think he's going to help us much here," I said.

"Not if you all keep using his name like that, damn," Maniac said.

"Have we managed to excise the wound to your satisfaction?" Virgil asked.

"Yeah," Ranger said.

"We were attempting – misguided as it may have been – to protect Meg," Virgil said.

Ranger grunted. "I think we know where those kinds of intentions lead."

"I feel like we're all ending up there anyway, so fuck it," Maniac said.

"That's a positive outlook," Ranger said.

She shrugged. "But realistic probably."

Ranger snorted. "Unlike the rest of you, I didn't go

around stealing cars and murdering—" he stopped and looked at me. "Sorry."

I looked down at the floor.

"Vengeance may have started hunting villains much sooner than even the military realized. In fact, I believe at that point you had stopped taking them out except for when opportunities presented themselves rather than finding them for yourself," Virgil said.

"I don't really…"

"Talk about it," Virgil finished kindly for me.

Greg wrapped an arm around my waist, drawing me against him. "Everyone responds to trauma differently," he reminded me.

"They weren't even villains," I said. "Just run-of-the-mill bad guys in the wrong place at the wrong time."

"Explains why they didn't just take you into custody at the time, though," Maniac said. "If they found roofies, well, it was just that things went very, very wrong, and you couldn't be blamed for your loss of control."

Ranger seemed to be thinking about it. "Why aren't you in custody?" he asked Maniac.

"Hey, yeah, what are your beans to spill?" I asked.

She snorted. "I'm not keeping any secrets, you can just Google anything I got charged with." She turned back to Ranger. "I got an official pardon. Had to do a six-month contract and hunt down some plant-powered asshole. He was strangling people with vines."

"All they signed you for was six months?" Greg asked.

"Yeah, why? How long was your contract for?"

"Last one was twenty-four months," Greg said. "They wanted to extend the next one to thirty-six."

"Couldn't trap you physically, so they were going to find a different way to do it," Virgil muttered.

"I can hear you," Greg said.

"You were meant to."

"What did they have you doing?" I asked.

"Helping local governments take out insurgents," Greg said. "I can find their bases faster than the military can, and I could be certain it only contained actual armed members of whichever group it was."

"Who determined who the insurgents were?"

"The local government," Greg said. "Bolt would give me a copy of the file on what was going on." He scrubbed at his face. "I don't know if—"

"For what's it worth," Virgil said, "I believe Bolt did do her best to ensure your morals wouldn't be compromised and did get them to assign you missions that were as clear cut as possible."

Greg grunted.

Virgil pulled out his phone. "It's getting late. We can either have a nice family dinner, or Ranger and Maniac can go patrol Royal Park to watch for Minotaurs."

Oh yeah, the brownstone district has a real neighborhood name. I just never remember it.

"Why not both?" Maniac said.

"Hey, has anyone fed Mirage?" I asked.

"He has food and water in the panic room with him," Virgil said, "but I will go check the security feeds to make sure he's staying put."

"Maybe we should all go," Greg said.

Virgil headed out Ranger's door without another word, and we all followed him up a floor to the security room down the hall across from Virgil's apartment. When we got there, Virgil flicked a hand, and the view on the monitors changed until it was the interior of one of the panic rooms.

"The cameras don't become active unless you put in a specific lockdown code," Virgil said, "so if for some reason one of you needed to retreat into a panic room, you need to enter in six-one-seven-five to have the cameras on."

Mirage wasn't there.

Virgil sighed, clicked a few buttons on the control board, and then spoke into the microphone on it. "Mirage, pull down the illusion please."

Nothing happened.

"He's in there, right?" Ranger asked.

Virgil rubbed the bridge of his nose. "Mirage, at the very least answer in the affirmative so we know you're alive."

Nothing.

"Could he have gotten out?" Greg asked.

"No. That code locks you in. You can't get out until someone puts in the code to let you out, and I didn't give him that code."

We all looked at Virgil.

"It's the same code just backwards," he told us. "You would've figured it out if I died."

"Could he have figured it out?" Greg pointed out.

"He didn't see the code get entered to start with," Virgil said.

"Well, we can't stand around staring at the monitor," Maniac said. "One of us should go check."

"On it," I said, turning to head out.

Behind me, both Greg and Ranger protested at the same time.

"Excuse me, but I think I've already proven I can break his illusions," I said.

"You're not going in by yourself," Greg said. "Ranger can go with you."

"How come Meg and I never get to team up?" Maniac asked. "We should get to go on an adventure together for a change."

"Next mission," Virgil said. "But for now, as Ranger is the only member immune to her compulsion, let's send him in with her. Also, I don't want you setting fire to the Tower."

We all trooped down to the floor below Ranger's, and then Greg, Virgil and Maniac hung back in the hallway while Ranger and I stepped into the apartment Virgil had set Mirage up in.

We must be really fond of studio style apartments

because it was another one of those.

Or maybe Virgil just wants to limit the number of hiding spaces available for anyone who might not belong here.

I didn't have to call the whispers because even though the panic room over by the kitchen was noticeably locked – there was a heavy steel door blocking the entrance – Mirage was sitting on the couch across from us, watching TV.

"Oh, hey, Meg," he said. "What's up, man?"

"Why aren't you in the panic room?" I asked.

"Thought one of you guys let me out. Door just opened up."

That I got a bad feeling about and called to the whispers, but as I was doing it, there was the crackle of electricity.

Mirage's face went pale, and he surged up off the couch just as something swung down onto the cushions, and what looked like little arcs of lightning went sizzling across the couch, leaving small flames in their wake.

Mirage charged in our direction. "Run, man!"

Ranger and I only stepped aside enough for Mirage to get past us, then the whispers settled on my shoulders, the momentary pause where they hadn't initially come to my call the only reason Mirage hadn't ended up running back the other way. Ranger and I backed up a bit to place ourselves in front of the door, the figures unfurling and swirling around us, shadows pooling on the floor, creeping their way out to the edge of my range before rising and swaying.

Nothing in the room moved. The crackling sound had stopped.

"Vengeance, I need you to move out of the room," Greg called from down the hallway.

"She's the only thing blocking whatever this is in," Ranger called back.

"I need her to come out. Vigilante is going to lock me in with them," Greg said calmly.

"Lock me in with who?" said a voice in the room. The crackle started again. "Bring it."

"Fortress," I said. "But I'm the one you need to be scared of."

"I can take you both."

The whispers were howling in my ears, and the figures started scratching their fingers along the floor, gouging out chunks of the wood. We stepped forward.

"Vengeance!" Greg yelled.

Footsteps, scurrying over toward the bedroom side of the apartment. We turned to face the sound.

Ranger stayed back, bodily blocking the way out. "Fortress, she's moving away from the door to give you room."

I wasn't, but I appreciated the cover.

"I don't want her going farther in!"

"You're going to argue this now?" Maniac said. "She's got it."

"Where's your baseball bat?" we asked Ranger.

"Garage," Ranger said.

We stepped toward the bedroom side, keeping our movements slow, languid. We had plenty of time for the hunt. But we had cleared the door enough that Greg could step into the room.

"Vengeance, don't move. I know who this is."

"Who?" we asked, turning to face him. Ranger caught our eyes too, and he winced, looking down at the floor.

Whoever it was on the other side did something stupid: they tried to charge us. They hit the edge of our range, and the figures lashed out, even as the crackle of electricity suddenly increased, sparks arcing off their fingers.

I felt it shudder up my legs, and I took a surprised step back.

"Poltergeist! Stop, she's pregnant!"

There was surprised silence, the sizzling in the air gone. Then, the voice: "Are you fucking kidding me?"

"No," Greg said. "Don't touch her. What's the contract for?"

"Why? You going to put in a bid on it?"

"Could someone explain what is going on?" Ranger said.

"I will, but not until Poltergeist comes out from hiding," Greg said. "Vengeance, could you please, please head out the door."

"I want to know how they got into the Tower to start with!" Virgil yelled from the hallway.

"Rode in on the back of the Humvee," the voice said. "Why are you sending pregnant heroes into the field?"

Greg made a frustrated noise. "I'm not."

"He does keep trying to stop us," we said.

"That's creepy," the voice said. "How many people you have in there, Vengeance?"

"Vengeance, let them go. We would like to all sit down like adults and discuss whatever the price on Mirage's head is," Virgil called down to us.

"No, no we wouldn't, man! I'm paying you to protect me, not have meetings!"

"Fine, first moves," the voice said. "Fortress, I'm coming out. Don't crush me."

A person appeared; they had backed up from the edge of my range, and they seemed to bloom into the air. They were androgynous – thin, dark haired, and light eyed, but that was all I could tell based on their build and facial features. They were holding a set of what looked like stun batons in their hands and dressed in what looked like white tactical armor. It had definitely seen some hard use based on the marks across the chest.

"Vengeance?" Greg said.

"Oh, right," I said, letting the whispers go. Greg crossed the room, placing himself between Poltergeist and me.

Poltergeist didn't miss that. They chuckled. "Oh, no. Fortress, you didn't."

Virgil and Maniac had come into the room, hanging back by the door with Ranger. Mirage was hollering from the hallway.

"Would you just end him please?" he was yelling.

"End *them*," Poltergeist said.

"Man, I don't give a fuck what your pronouns are!" Mirage yelled. "You just tried to kill me!"

I snorted. "Probably wouldn't care either way."

"Villains rarely do," Poltergeist said. "I seem to have missed quite a few things while I was out of town," they commented to Greg.

"You did," Greg said warily. "Where were you?"

"South America. Nice little village down there. I would tell you where, but things are a bit, heated, in the area."

"Seriously, what the fuck is going on?" Ranger asked. "We just had a talk about this."

"Poltergeist is a – well, not an assassin exactly," Greg said. I had never heard Greg hedge like that before.

"Mercenary," Poltergeist said. "My services are for hire for any and all targets."

"They specialize in infiltration," Greg said.

"How do you know Fortress?" Maniac asked.

"Drinking buddies," Poltergeist said.

"Fortress doesn't drink," I said.

"He really shouldn't," Poltergeist said. "How many bars did we break?"

Greg cleared his throat. "I only put a hole in the one."

"That was not a hole. That was a—" Poltergeist paused and thought about it, their head tilted. "Crater. That was a crater."

"Was there even a bar left?" Maniac asked.

"I believe you can play catch up later," Virgil said. "What's the price on Mirage?"

"Five hundred," Poltergeist said.

"Mirage, if you're hoping to do a payoff you're on your own," Virgil called out.

"What the fuck, man!"

"I can't outbid that price," Virgil said. "I don't have the resources for that."

"So just murder him!"

"Them," Poltergeist corrected.

"Man, fuck you!"

"I get that a lot," Poltergeist said. "So, Fortress, what will it be? Because you know I'll take her out if it means I get my target."

"Who hired you?" Virgil said.

Poltergeist chuckled. "I don't give up my clients. If we're done here, I have a job to do."

"Then we have a problem," Virgil said, "because I don't give up my clients either."

"Everyone out but Fortress and me," Maniac said. "The two of us will handle them."

Poltergeist chuckled again. "You're all cute."

"Wait," Greg said.

"For?" Poltergeist asked.

"Old times sake," Greg said.

Poltergeist tilted their head again. "You for hire this time? I've got a target that's bigger than I usually handle."

"Civilians?" Greg asked.

"None. Some drug lord down in Central America, but it's the whole compound. What's your price? Because I'm not splitting it more than eighty-twenty, so don't even ask."

"Ten if you give up who put the contract out on Mirage and don't touch my team," Greg said.

"That's – you know you're supposed to haggle for more, right? That's how negotiations work," Poltergeist said. "And I'm not giving up the five I'm getting for him."

"He's faked his death before; he can do it again," Greg said.

"Not going to work. I'm supposed to bring back his head as proof."

Greg was thinking. I could see how tense the muscles along his back were. "Mirage, if we get you a head, can you put an illusion on it?"

"Yes!"

"You think they're not going to check for that?"

127

Poltergeist said. "I think they want to display it."

"What do you care?" Mirage yelled. "Just give him the damn client's name so these idiots can get paid to take them out!"

"If word gets out that I gave up a client, I'll never work again," Poltergeist said.

"Man, I'm not going to tell anyone! I'm going to go back to being dead in peace!"

"We're not snitches," Maniac said.

"Where are you getting a head from?" Poltergeist asked.

Greg sighed, pulled out his phone, scrolled, tapped, and held it up to his ear. "White," he said when she answered. "I need one of the skulls."

CHAPTER NINE

White demanded we come down to the morgue and explain why we wanted a skull from one of the victims.

Poltergeist stated that they were staying wherever Mirage was.

Mirage protested he was not staying wherever Poltergeist was.

As Fortress was the only one on the team Poltergeist trusted not to change the rules of the game on them, they insisted Fortress was staying wherever they were.

Greg argued that he was not leaving me without him but also didn't want me around Poltergeist. Because honestly, if it came down to protecting me or protecting Mirage, we all knew who was going to win that one. And Greg didn't trust Poltergeist not to use that to their advantage.

We spent a while going around in circles, while Ranger kept inserting snide comments about still not explaining things. Maniac told him to shut it and let us get the whole thing worked out first before we got into the history lesson.

Eventually Greg sighed, texted White that we were having technical difficulties, and said he might have to bring the whole team plus a couple extras.

When the text pinged back, Greg looked surprised. "She said that's fine."

"Fabulous," Virgil said briskly. "We need to arrange transport."

"I'll just fly Vengeance and me in, and we'll meet the rest of you there," Greg said.

"Uh, no, *we*," Poltergeist said, making a circle motion with their index finger, "are all going together."

"I don't have a vehicle with that kind of room," Virgil said.

"I could take Maniac on the bike," Ranger offered.

"I am not riding in the same vehicle as that–" Mirage started hotly.

"Enough!" Virgil said. "Hummer, everyone. Mirage, passenger side. Vengeance, you're behind him. Maniac, driver side. I don't care if the rest of you walk."

"I'm not—" Greg started.

"Then ride in the middle," Virgil snapped.

"I'm going with you," Poltergeist said.

"Trunk," Virgil said.

"I'm taking the bike," Ranger said.

"Good," Virgil said. "At least someone here makes decisions."

There was another hold up at the elevator. "I'm not riding down with him, man," Mirage said.

"Them," Poltergeist patiently corrected him again.

"Man, I already said—"

Greg had had enough. He grabbed Mirage's arm, twisting it up behind his back, and shoving him onto the elevator. "Shut up."

"Ow! Ow, man! Come on! I'm going!"

The rest of us followed, Greg planting himself between Mirage and me, an arm slung over my shoulders. Mirage glowered at us from the back corner. Poltergeist slipped in ahead of Virgil, positioning themselves in the corner across from Mirage, their back to the front of the elevator, arms crossed as they leaned back against the wall. They had their batons holstered on their hips, where they had put them since Greg had called White.

Maniac ended up next to me, her eyes on Poltergeist. Ranger was in front of us next to Virgil, who had taken up a position in front of the buttons.

"So," Ranger said. "This isn't awkward at all."

I snickered.

It was a good thing it was a short elevator ride because it was exceedingly uncomfortable with how tense everyone was.

When we got to the Hummer, that was when the seating arrangements got rethought.

"Front," Virgil said to Poltergeist.

"I thought I was in the trunk," they said.

"I'm switching you and Mirage."

Greg made an irritated sound. "That doesn't change the line of sight between Mirage and Poltergeist."

Virgil was rubbing both his eyes. "Can we not argue over this again?"

"Don't trust me, Fortress?" Poltergeist said.

"No, I don't," Greg said.

"Fair enough," they said, and they pulled the batons out of their holsters. Everyone tensed, but all they did was flip them over, and hold them out handle first. "You hold onto these. A gesture of good faith."

Greg hesitated. Poltergeist gave the batons a little shake, and Greg reached for them, then paused again, his eyes narrowed. "Don't do it."

Poltergeist sighed, set the batons down on the garage floor and stepped back from them.

"Good," Virgil said. "Get in the trunk."

"Now I'm back in the trunk?"

"People who try to electrocute my people don't get seats with a belt."

"It wouldn't have hurt him," Poltergeist said, but they climbed into the back of the Hummer once Virgil had pulled the door open.

Greg turned to me. "You're going with Ranger."

"What?" Ranger and I both said.

"I'm not having you in the car with them."

"Thought you two you were drinking buddies," Ranger said.

"Yeah, that doesn't make us friends," Greg said. "They will take out anyone in their way to get their target. I don't want Vengeance caught in the middle."

"Oh, no, Fortress, buddy. She's riding with us," Poltergeist said from where they were half hanging out. "I want to know all about the woman who caught you."

Greg stepped between us.

"We," Virgil said, "are wasting time. Fortress, in the trunk; Ranger, middle; Vengeance, Maniac, Mirage, same spots."

It takes a while for Virgil to lose patience, and he had reached that point.

Greg planted himself against the back of the rear seats, placing himself firmly between Poltergeist and the rest of us. He might have shoved them out of his way just a bit.

Ranger settled, kneeling on the metal hump between the seats, facing Poltergeist.

Which left Maniac and I to watch Mirage while Virgil drove us.

There was a startled swear from the rear when Virgil gassed it, and the Hummer roared forward, tires thundering as he swung us out in traffic.

Greg chuckled. "Might want to hold on."

Ranger, for his part, had almost toppled into me. "Watch the road!" he shot over his shoulder.

"Who gave him a license?" Poltergeist asked.

Maniac had twisted around. "How'd you two meet?"

"Mission," Greg grunted.

"I got hired by a client, and we just happened to have the same target for different reasons," Poltergeist said.

"Poltergeist had taken it out before I got there," Greg said, "and when I arrived, they attacked me."

"How'd that work out for you?" Maniac asked

Poltergeist.

"Poorly," they said. "I hadn't realized he could hear me."

"How'd that lead to a bar getting destroyed?" Ranger asked.

"You punch each other a few times, you end up friends," Poltergeist said.

"You electrocuted me," Greg said.

"You were fine."

"I was tasting metal for a week after."

"If you're going to hold a grudge here, then I would like to point out you broke my jaw."

"You were fine," Greg said.

"What was that – your first mission?" Poltergeist asked. "Because it showed."

Greg chuckled.

"May I remind you? Dude is trying to kill me," Mirage said from the front.

"Yeah, except I like them," Greg said.

"Thought you weren't friends," Ranger said.

"Not right now we're not," Greg said.

"I must have hit a sore spot," Poltergeist said. "I don't remember you being this sensitive."

"You threatened my wife."

"I seem to recall you saying you weren't the marrying type," Poltergeist said. "I must have missed a *lot*."

Virgil discretely reached a hand back, so the palm was facing Ranger. Maniac and I braced, and then Virgil hit the brakes. The Hummer came to a sudden stop, rocking a bit, and Poltergeist slid with it, crashing into the back of the seats, Greg had dodged out of their way, bracing himself against my seat and the side of the car. Ranger was the only one who hadn't moved with the car, although he had grabbed the back of the seats in front of him.

"Ow," I said, because I had been flung into the seatbelt.

"Vigilante!" Greg snapped.

"Oops. Wrong person. Sorry, Vengeance," Virgil said.

"Oh, so you wanted *me* going through the windshield?" Ranger asked.

Greg was already moving though, picking Poltergeist up off the floor of the trunk, pulling them out of the car, and slamming them against the side of the Hummer. "Stay," he said, before flinging open my car door, yanking the seatbelt off me, and settling his ear against my stomach.

"Hi," I said. He had one hand up on my shoulder, the other on my thighs, and I felt his fingers flex as he sighed.

"Hi," he said. He stepped back and helped me out of the car. Poltergeist had stayed where Greg had shoved them, and they were watching us.

"What?" I said.

"When did you get married?" they asked.

"Couple months ago," Greg said.

"When did you meet?"

"Catch up later," Virgil said, coming around to us. "We have a meeting." Ranger and Maniac came around with him.

"I'm staying right here," Mirage said through the passenger side window. "I am not going anywhere he's going."

Virgil had his hand back at his eyes. "Oh, just fucking kill him."

"Whoa! Wait, man, I'm coming, I'm coming," Mirage said, scrambling out of the Hummer.

The morgue was a squat, brick building, a few windows on the front, and alleys on either side of it leading around to the back. We headed in the front door, and the lobby was a mix of beige and green speckled linoleum flooring. The only seating was a couple of hard plastic chairs, the space too small to comfortably fit the number of people we had. The greying woman – and I do mean greying, her hair was grey, her skin had a greyish cast to it, even the whites of her eyes looked grey – at reception stared at us.

"Can I help you?" she asked. Even her voice sounded grey.

I really hoped it was the lighting because she didn't look healthy.

"Fortress, Vengeance, Vigilante, Ranger, Maniac and guests here to see Detective White," Greg told her.

"Oookay," she said, picking up a phone, and punching a couple buttons. "Doctor Frank, there's a bunch of – heroes – here, to see you and Detective White." She listened for a moment, then nodded and hung up. "You can go on back. Doctor Frank's office is down the hall to the right, third door on the left," she said and hit the release for the door leading further into the building. It buzzed.

Virgil was the closest to it, so he yanked it open and made Mirage step through first. Poltergeist slid in after him, but Ranger and Maniac stepped through, placing themselves between the two.

"I'm not going to do anything at the morgue," Poltergeist said.

Greg and I came through, and Virgil was last. The door slammed shut behind us, locking again. Virgil led the way down the hallway, and at the door to Frank's office, he paused and looked back at us.

"We may need to do this in the hall," he said.

Dr. Frank, a black man with short hair, had poked his head out, but when he saw how many people there were, he stepped into the hallway itself. He was as tall as Greg was, matching him for sheer bulk, but where Greg was all coiled energy, Dr. Frank gave off a very similar vibe to Dr. Hawk, calm and controlled, his movements smooth.

"You're not the coroner," I said, the words popping out of my mouth before I thought them through.

"I'm the medical examiner," Frank said, with a tight, professional smile.

Greg had laid a hand on my shoulder. "Vengeance is new to all this."

White had come out into the hall. "He's the one you need to explain why you need a skull," she said. "Don't hold it against her," she said addressing Frank. "She met Beetle."

"Ah," Frank said. "Why do you need one of the victim's skulls?"

Greg was watching him quietly. "You've already decided you're not going to give us one."

Frank looked startled for a moment. "Yes, I had decided that."

"Then why have us come down here?"

Frank crossed his arms. "White said I should give you a chance to convince me."

Greg was still watching him. "That seems like it's going to be a waste of both our time."

"Probably would be," Frank said agreeably.

"Man, seriously?" Mirage said. "Just move him out of your way."

Greg shot him a look. "I don't work that way."

"Tough luck," Poltergeist said. "I'll just take my target and be on my way."

"No," Greg said. "Different solution."

"Why are you protecting him?" Poltergeist asked. "He's a villain. It's not like he's a contributing member of society."

"Retired villain," Mirage said.

"Villains don't retire," Poltergeist said, shooting a glance in Maniac's direction. She ignored them.

Greg scrubbed at his face. "We owe him."

"I really did miss a lot," Poltergeist said. "What have you been getting up to?"

"I went freelance," Greg said.

"As entertaining as this glimpse into hero life is," White said. "If you could wait here a moment." She marched off down the hallway through a door at the end.

Frank went after her. "White! White, where are you going?" She came back through the doors, one of the skulls in a clear, sealed plastic bag. "Don't – where are you going with that?" he asked, matching her pace. It looked like he didn't want to physically stop her.

She stopped in front of us, held the bag up. "Is getting this going to help you get rid of whatever is eating people?"

"You have a cannibal in the city?" Poltergeist asked.

"Something like that," Maniac said.

"Oh, count me in," Poltergeist said, "but only if I get my five."

"Yes," Virgil lied. "It will." White handed him the bag.

"Try to bring it back," she said. "The family is going to want to have the whole body to bury."

∞

We still hadn't eaten, and Ranger and Maniac still needed to go patrol Royal Park to see if any Minotaurs showed up.

Virgil ended up calling in an order for pizza, and we picked it up on the way back to the Tower. He made Greg and Poltergeist hold the boxes on the way home where they sat in the trunk because Mirage was up front again holding the skull.

There was momentary hesitation at the elevator because Greg was carrying all the pizzas, and Poltergeist snagged their batons back off the floor of the garage, and Greg was still trying to block the space between them and me.

Virgil had decided it for him by herding everybody onto the elevator past him so that his only choice at that point was to step on and stand in the middle.

Poltergeist had backed up into the farthest corner, and I was over on the other side of the elevator from them, which might be the only reason why Greg didn't hand the pizzas to someone else.

We only went up to the floor Virgil had placed Mirage on and into the apartment that he had been staying in. When we got in there, Virgil examined the scorch marks on the couch.

"You're paying for that," he said.

"You're going to make me pay for the couch?" Poltergeist asked.

"He will," Greg said, settling the pizzas on the kitchen

island and separating boxes from the stack. "Are the plates in the same place?"

"Yes," Virgil said.

Maniac started pulling plates out of the cabinet and setting them next to the pizza boxes.

Mirage was standing in the middle of the room holding the skull. "Look, man, can I just do this and hand it over so he – they – can go?"

"Feel free to get started," Virgil said, "but my team has ongoing missions, so we can't just stop everything for you."

"Fucking heroes," Mirage grumbled, but settled the skull down on the coffee table, ripping the bag open and taking it out. He sat examining it for a moment before setting it back down on the coffee table, and then leaned over, staring at it.

"What are you doing?" I asked.

"It needs some physical characteristics. I can't just make hair magically appear, man. Wait, that came out wrong. It needs a wig so that way when someone picks it up, they think it's a real head."

"It is a real head," I said.

Mirage waved me off. "Look, I can trick the senses into feeling skin under their fingers, I can trick them into feeling hair, but if there's no hair there to grab a hold of, I can't imitate that. I can't add things that aren't there." He thought about it for a second. "Get it, man?"

"No," I said, just to be frustrating. "You add things that aren't there all the time."

Mirage opened his mouth, spotted Greg watching him, and rethought whatever he was about to say to me. I smirked at him. He glared back. "Look, man, I need a wig or a toupee. Someone get me one."

"How are you planning on attaching it?" Virgil asked.

"Glue?" Mirage said.

Virgil set down his plate and headed out the door. The stairwell door opened and closed.

While we were waiting for whatever it was Virgil had

gone to fetch, Greg came around, wrapped an arm around my waist, and turned me and steered me over to the island, settling me on a stool next to Maniac. "You should eat," he said gently.

The smell made my stomach turn over, and I shook my head, swiveling on my stool to face the other way. Which, no, this is not fair. It's Malus City-style pizza. From the pizzeria down the block from us, which has the best.

Well, the best to me. There's a lot of arguing and competition between the pizzerias and the city dwellers over who makes the best pizza in downtown. We all agreed on one thing: Garro and their deep dish can suck it.

Greg put a hand on my back, rubbing circles. "Just breathe."

"I am breathing," I said.

Maniac had paused in her eating. "Just don't barf on me."

That made me laugh, which didn't help my stomach. "Oh, don't do that."

Mirage was watching us. "What's going on? Don't get me sick."

Oh right, Mirage was in the hall when Greg had announced I was pregnant to Poltergeist. He must not have heard it from where he was. It had sounded like he was yelling from as far down as he could get.

"What are you, dense?" Maniac asked. "Fortress only yelled it out like, five times."

"Once," Greg said. "I said it once."

"Oh shit, man, are you pregnant?" Mirage said.

"Someone give him a cookie," I said through gritted teeth.

"How'd you even miss that?" Maniac said. "It's been all over the news with speculation for the last twenty-four hours."

"Panic room," Mirage said. "There's no TV in there."

"I suppose I could remedy that," Virgil said, coming back in. He was carrying a blond wig and a tube of Gorilla Glue, and he set them down on the coffee table in front of

Mirage.

"How are you planning on removing the wig when you get the skull back to White?" Greg asked.

"Carefully."

Mirage was ignoring us at this point, having settled the wig on the skull. He was carefully sliding it around until he had it placed the way he wanted, and then he opened the bottle of glue and began slowly and methodically gluing the wig down sections at a time.

"Stop watching me, man, it's making me nervous," he said.

Greg's phone rang, and I think all of us twitched a bit, even Poltergeist, who had been quietly standing in a corner created by the counters and cabinets while they ate.

Greg pulled out his phone, swore, then answered it anyway. "Hey, Mom," he sighed. "Yes, I talked to her about dinner, but we've been working and haven't—" he paused and sighed again. "Hold on." He pulled the phone away from his ear. "My mom wants to go to dinner tomorrow night."

"Just her?"

"No," he said.

I thought about it for a minute, then turned to Maniac. "Band-aid?" I asked.

"Band-aid," she agreed.

"Fine," I said to Greg.

He put the phone back to his face. "Yeah, we can make that. Where and what time?" He listened for a moment. "Yeah, see you there. Love you too." He hung up, and slipped the phone back into his pocket.

"Where are you going for dinner?" Poltergeist asked.

"Not telling you," Greg said.

"I'll be back out of town at that point," Poltergeist pointed out. "Not like I'll be crashing the party."

"Still not telling you."

"Thought you were going to help with the cannibal situation," Ranger said.

"Oh, I am, but I've got to go drop the head off first. That's going to take me a couple days. Some of us can't fly around the world in minutes."

"It's not minutes," Greg said. "It takes longer than that."

"What's your record?" Poltergeist asked.

Greg rubbed the back of his neck. "Less than twenty-four hours? I didn't time it."

"You ever tell them about the time you raced the Blackbird?"

Greg cleared his throat. "No. And it wasn't a fair race; they should've gotten a head start."

"You're going to have to explain this," Ranger said.

"I can take off faster than the jet, since I don't need a runway," Greg said. "So, they should've been given, what? A five, ten second head start? Especially with the refuel happening right then."

"At that point you're both in the air. I don't see how they would need one."

"Why were you racing a jet to start with?" Ranger asked.

"We had a bet going," Poltergeist said. "I was working with a crew that was cooperating with the military, and Fortress was part of the team they sent. The normies were curious about what he could do."

"There just happened to be a jet there?" Ranger asked.

"Well, we were on the base," Poltergeist said.

"How did you convince your superiors that was going to be a good use of resources?" Virgil asked.

Greg rubbed the back of his neck. "They had been drinking with us."

"You drunk flew?" Ranger asked.

"Drunk raced," Greg said. "I hit a mountain."

"But you still won," Poltergeist said.

"Still wrecking, just not cars?" I asked.

Greg grinned at me. "I haven't wrecked in a long time."

"What constitutes a long time?" I asked.

"What's it been – three, four years?" Poltergeist asked.

"Can't remember," Greg said.

"Probably all the mountains you hit," Ranger said.

Mirage had finished gluing the wig down and had come over, snagging a slice of pizza and no plate. He took his slice over to the couch.

"If you get grease on that, you're paying for it," Virgil said.

"Thought that asshole was paying for it already," Mirage said, motioning at Poltergeist.

"Yes, but the damage they caused was incidental. Yours is preventable by the subtle application of a plate."

"Whatever, man," Mirage said, his mouth full.

CHAPTER TEN

By the time Mirage was done setting up the illusion, Ranger and Maniac had already headed out, which left Virgil, Greg, Poltergeist and I sitting with him.

He spent a minute turning the head in circles, examining it.

"What are you doing now?" I asked.

"I have to make sure it looks good," he said. "Is the blood leaking out of the mouth too much? I've got it there. The ears, the nose – it's too much, isn't it?"

"You might want to add some scorches, since I would've just electrocuted you to start with." Poltergeist told him.

Mirage muttered to himself but made the adjustments. "There. A real work of art, man." He picked it up by the hair and gave it a jiggle. "Wig seems good to stay." He held it out. "Here. All done."

Watching the subject of the illusion hold out his own dismembered head like it was no big deal was kind of a weird thing to witness.

Poltergeist took it, hefted it up, and looked it in the face. "Really good work on the eyes. How long is this going to last?"

"Until I take it off, so it'll stay indefinitely."

"Your client's name?" Virgil asked.

"No. You're not getting that until after I get back. I

need to get paid first, and you're going to need to give it a while before you go after them. Give it some time so no one connects me to their death. And in the meantime, Fortress can help me with my other contract."

"You're going to give us that information before I've helped you?" Greg asked warily.

"You're good for it," Poltergeist said. "Well, this has been entertaining and informative. I'm going to go. I'll let you know when I'm on my way back, and we can catch up on our Central America trip."

"I'll escort you out," Virgil said.

"Fortress can see me to the door if you're that paranoid about making sure I leave."

Greg sighed. "Come on then." The two of them headed out the door.

"Mirage," Virgil said. "I would like to set you up in a different panic room for safety's sake."

"Yeah, man, sounds good to me. I don't trust that fucker."

"Meg, if you would come with us, please?"

I hopped off the stool, and the three of us headed out the door and up a floor. Virgil went into the apartment next door to Ranger's and sighed.

There was extra furniture in the room, neatly lined up over by the bed.

"What, you're putting me in storage?" Mirage asked.

"Apparently," Virgil said, motioning at the panic room. "If you could."

Mirage rolled his eyes, but headed into the room, and Virgil flicked his hand, the door to the room hiss-slamming behind Mirage.

"Where's the keypad?" I asked.

Virgil caught my eye and motioned for me to follow him. I did, and he led me up to security, then closed the door behind us. "There are two keypads. One is inside the room; the other is hidden at the back of the kitchen cabinets. I had to change the code for that one since I don't know that Poltergeist won't sneak their way back in."

"They've got their head," I said.

"But technically not their target," Virgil pointed out. "I don't know how well that will sit with them."

"They're still getting paid."

"Hmm, yes, and Greg could tell me if they are, in fact, going to stick to this. But I couldn't ask him in front of them."

"You couldn't just read their thoughts?" I asked.

"Part of their power appears to be camouflaging those. Their mind is quite literally a blank spot for me."

"Oh," I said.

Virgil opened the door back up. "Yes, oh. Fortunately, Greg can hear their heartbeat and their movements."

Down the hall, we could hear footsteps, and we both straightened up as Greg poked his head in.

"They're gone," he said.

"Good," Virgil said. "I am retiring to my apartment. I recommend you two do the same until we hear from Ranger and Maniac." He slipped past Greg at the door, and I heard his door open and shut.

Greg stepped into the room and wrapped his arms around me, his nose in my hair.

"I thought we were going to the apartment," I said.

"In a minute," he said, his arms tightening. We stood there silently, my head resting against him. After a long moment, he scooped me up.

"What are you doing?" I asked.

"Carrying you," he said.

"I can walk, you know," I teased.

"I know."

"Is this more of your taking care of me stuff?"

"Yes," he said quietly. He headed down the hall to the apartment and swung the door open, stepped inside and shut and locked it behind us.

Greg carried me past the entry and past the living room

while I was trying to look around. The apartment looked like the set up was similar to Virgil's, but as we went past another room, it appeared to have a second bedroom rather than the library he had in his.

Greg took me into the master bedroom, settled me on the bed, and started unlacing my shoes.

"You know I can take my own shoes off," I said.

"Meg," he said, looking up at me. "Can you please—"

But I didn't let him finish his sentence, because I pulled my foot free, swung my legs away, so I could scoot down next to him and kissed him.

I felt him relax beside me, his hands coming up, sliding under my shirt, his fingers slipping gently along my skin, brushing their way up my ribs, stopping just too low.

I made a noise, and he chuckled, pulled back, and lifted my shirt off. Then his lips were on my neck, his breath tickling my skin, his hands again too low. I plucked at his shirt, and he moved just enough to peel it off himself and toss it on the floor before his lips were on my skin, grazing their way down my shoulder.

He slid me further back onto the bed, nestling me against the pillows, one hand skimming along my leg, even as he trailed kisses down my neck and shoulder. Then he pulled away, and his focus changed.

"I am taking off your shoes," he said.

"Hmm," I said. "Are you now?" I tried to pull my foot away again, but he had his fingers wrapped around my ankle.

"You're not to going to win this one, cheating or not," he teased. He had the laces undone, pulled my shoe free, and dropped it on the floor.

I moved my other foot away from him.

"You're going to make me chase you?" he asked.

"Are you going to catch me?"

His eyes had turned serious. "Meg, as long as you want me to, I will."

"Always," I said.

He smiled at me and moved before I was expecting it so that he was pressed against me, his weight pinning me in place. Slowly, he reached down, grabbed my leg by the calf, and very gently bent my knee so he could reach my foot without having to get off me.

For once, it didn't pop, or the whole moment might have been ruined.

Look, it's one thing for me to ruin it on my own, but that stupid kneecap better shut up.

He pulled my other shoe free while I was busy fretting over my knee keeping its lousy opinion to itself. His hand was gliding up my leg, his lips back on mine. His other hand had slipped under my head, his fingers tangled in my curls.

"Meg," was all he said.

∞

He had turned off the lights at some point and was drawing circles on my back. I could almost feel him brooding next to me, and I didn't want to ask what was bothering him.

I didn't have to.

"I have to tell you something," he said, and it sounded like a confession, which made me tense. His hand stilled against me, the palm resting warm between my shoulder blades, his fingers just brushing the back of my neck.

"What?" I asked when the silence stretched and he didn't seem inclined to say anything further.

"I'm taking on your debt when Poseidon decides he wants you to pay up."

"I don't know that it's transferable," I said cautiously, afraid he might go running off to find Ares or even Bacchus so he could find out.

"I looked up some of the tales, Meg. They've done it before."

I could feel my heart clench, and I sat up. His hand fell away from my back, and I reached behind me and grabbed it, pulled it to my chest, my hands clinging to his. "Greg—" I said, and that had his attention, his fingers flexing in mine, because as often as he says my name, I rarely say his to him, "I don't know what the price is. Can we at least find out the price before you start offering yourself up? What if it's something only the Furies can do? What if it's something you won't do? Would you go that far for me?"

"Yes," he said, simply, no hesitation. I didn't know which question he had just answered, and I was afraid to ask. I didn't get a chance to make a decision as to which way I wanted to go, because he kissed me, his hands back on me, and I gave myself over to the urgency in his touch, because in truth, I don't think I wanted to know.

But I wouldn't let him compromise who he was for me.

∞

A phone was ringing in the dark.

At some point, we had dozed off, Greg's ear resting against my stomach. When he laid his head there, I had teased him about it, but he told me listening to our heartbeats together was soothing.

I was closer, so I picked the phone up off the nightstand, squinting at the screen, pushing at Greg's shoulder as I answered it. "Ranger?"

"Meg? Why are you answering attack dog's phone?" His voice was so quiet, I could barely hear the words, the phone pressed to my ear as if pushing it closer would help.

"I was closer to it."

Greg sat up and held out his hand, and I handed him the phone. "Ranger," he said. He listened for a moment. "Hold on, I'm putting this on speaker so Meg can hear." He did, turning the volume up for me as well. "You're a go."

"We didn't find any Minotaurs, but we did run across a group of something. Meg needs to come down and see these."

"Can you describe them?" I asked.

"Maniac barbecued them pretty good, so, no, not really. I think we need you specifically."

He was dancing around the subject, which wasn't like Ranger. "What happened?" I asked.

"One of them – well, all of them – tried to bite me. They swarmed. I think we have more than one thing eating people."

"Give me the cross streets you're at," Greg said.

"Hare and Fox."

"Give us—" his eyes flicked down, fastened on my stomach, "damn it, it's going to take us a bit. I can't go full speed right now."

I hopped of the bed, snagging my clothes back off the floor. "I think you can go a little bit faster than you think you can."

"Speed of a car," Greg reminded me.

"You get here when you get here," Ranger said, and he hung up.

Greg had gotten off the bed too and was grabbing his clothes. We dressed in silence, and then Greg opened up our suitcase and pulled something out, giving it a shake and holding it out to me. "Here."

It was the jacket Ranger had given me. "What is that for?" I asked.

"It's reinforced. It's not going to stop anything big, but it should slow down anything with teeth."

I took it and slipped it on. "They're not going to be able to get near me to begin with."

Greg had pulled his shoes on, then stepped up to me, got the jacket zipped, and settled a hand on my face, his thumb brushing my cheek. "No, they won't."

He scooped me up, hurrying us through the apartment, up the stairs and into our apartment so we could exit via the balcony. He paused. He had left the lights on when he had come back up to get us the things we needed, so we could clearly see it sitting on the kitchen island: a basket of wine and grapes. "What the fuck is that?"

"It looks like a gift," I said, trying to squirm out of his grasp to go look.

His fingers tightened against me. "Well, we can check it out later. First things first." He headed us out the balcony door and shut it carefully behind us with a muttered, "Not that that will stop them," and leapt us into the air.

∞

Ranger and Maniac were both noticeably tense when we got there. She was balancing on the balls of her feet, one arm swinging, hand flexing, while the other hand held the protein bar she was eating. Ranger was doing the thing where he looks like he's relaxed, but he's not, because he's leaning against a wall, arms crossed, one foot up, ready to come off it.

The remains on the sidewalk and street were definitely extra crispy.

Greg set me down next to Maniac, and Ranger came off the wall to stand with us. We stared at the bodies for a moment.

"You said they swarmed and tried to bite you?" Greg asked.

"Yeah," Ranger said. "They almost took a chunk of Maniac because they came out of nowhere. They didn't manage to get one off me, but they fucked up my jacket. Look at this thing." He held out an arm, shaking the sleeve out a bit. They had definitely put long gaping tears in the leather.

"You alright?" Greg asked Maniac.

"Fine," she said. "I just flamed up when the first one jumped me. I'm going to need to stop at an all-night diner or something, though. Their skin is pretty tough."

"Meg?" Greg said. I nodded, calling to the whispers, and even as Greg and Maniac took hurried steps back from me, Ranger stepped forward. Together, we walked over to the blackened things. The whispers were brushing against my shoulders, the figures flowing down my arms, and the shadows had pooled at my feet, their inky blackness swirling against the body I knelt over. It was lying on its side, the body contorted, hands and legs pulled up into a fetal position, the fingers like claws.

I took another look: the fingers were claws. At least, toward the end the last knuckle ended in hooked talons. There were only four fingers. They reminded me of a bird of prey with the shape of them, the thumb too far toward the wrist of the arm to be human.

Were we dealing with Harpies? They were supposed to be part bird, but I could see no evidence of wings on what was left of these things.

I looked down at the feet: four toes. At least, as far as I could tell. Parts of the bodies looked melted together, as if the skin had run like hot wax.

"It's definitely the people eater from the second scene," I said to Greg, and I could hear the echo of the whispers in my voice.

I was trying to look over the face, but here, on all of them, the skin had again melted and run down, exposing the bone of the skull at the top, scorched and burnt. There weren't any identifying features to tell me what they were.

"What kind of look did you get at them?" I asked.

"Not a good enough one," Ranger said. "Maniac lit that group up too quickly, and I was busy getting the hell out of dodge before one of them ate me to check it out."

"You didn't slow it?" Greg asked.

"I did, and the moment I got free of it, Maniac set it on fire. I wasn't going to stick around asking it about its characteristics."

Greg grunted.

I was trying to listen to the whispers, but they couldn't tell me much more. They still considered it easy prey. I wasn't so sure they were right.

"Where'd you park the bike?" Greg was asking when his

phone rang. He pulled it out, and the look on his face turned grim. "White. You have another scene, don't you?" He winced, and I knew she was yelling. "No, we ran across a second monster. There's more than one of them. Give me the address you're at." He listened for a moment. "We're in the area already. We'll be there in just a few." Then hung up. He looked at me as he slipped the phone back into his pocket. "It's just up the street."

"How many this time?" I asked.

"Only two. Might be why they attacked Ranger and Maniac in the street."

"They were still hungry."

"Where's the bike?" Greg repeated.

"Down that way," Ranger said, pointing down to his left.

"Okay, can you and Maniac retrieve it and meet us at 45 Hare? It's a couple blocks up, so we'll just walk."

Ranger jerked his head, and he and Maniac trotted off down the street away from us.

Greg turned to me. "Can you let them go?" he asked, but the whispers had already faded, and I was stepping toward him. He wrapped an arm around my waist, and we headed down the street in the opposite direction of Ranger and Maniac.

It only took us about ten minutes to get up the street to where White was. She had called us even before the coroner, so it was her, any officers she had with her, and the CSI van.

We had even managed to beat the news team.

The growl of an approaching engine, and Ranger and Maniac were pulling up to the curb, climbing off the bike and meeting us at the steps.

White was glaring at us from the door. "Thought you said the skull would help you stop whatever is doing this," she said.

"It's two monsters," I said.

"So, kill the two of them," she snapped at me.

"Vengeance means it's two different types of monsters," Greg said.

White went grey. "Two different types? We have two different types of monsters that eat people?"

Greg scrubbed at his face. "Yes, and this one hunts in packs. The other one is solitary. Hopefully we've gotten all of them taken out."

I'm not sure White could've looked any sicker than she already did, but somehow, she managed it, her skin fully ashen, jaw clenched, and she swallowed hard before she spoke. "If I report that there's a second monster, they're going to turn this over to the feds."

Greg sighed. "That'll end any cooperation we're getting on the law enforcement side. It'll become a military operation." He looked like he was thinking. "We may want to do that. Vigilante is used to working around them; he'll know how to make sure we stay involved."

White nodded. "I'll include it in my report then."

"For now, can we come look at the scene?" Greg asked.

"Yeah, they were on the first floor, front room this time," White said, turning and heading into the building. The four of us followed. She was barely into the brownstone before she turned to the right, motioning us through a door. Greg started to step through, then blocked the room with his arm.

"Fuck," he said. "You said two. This doesn't look like two."

I peeked around him. There was blood pooled over the floor, splashed up the walls, the kills much messier than the previous ones. They hadn't even finished; there were still entrails spilled across the wood planks, muscle clinging to the bone. "Fortress," I said. "Let us in." I could feel the whispers, plucking at me.

Greg looked down at me and stepped back out of my way. The whispers didn't wait for anything more, and I saw White shudder and back up down the hall as we stepped into the room.

I was going to be tracking footprints back out of the room. That's how far the blood had crept toward the door.

The figures and shadows moved forward, the figures' fingers making trails in the congealing blood. The whispers sighed in my ears, and I closed my eyes, listening to what they were saying. "It's two victims," I said. "We've done damage like this ourselves. They were – interrupted."

"By what?" Greg's voice. I could hear the tremor and hoped White missed it.

The smell of brine in the air, a memory of it in the room, the whispers could sense it. My eyes popped open, my heart sped up, and Greg heard it.

"Vengeance, by what?" his voice had sharpened, overriding the fear.

"They're one of his," the whispers and I said, leaving it up to Greg to interpret that.

I heard him swearing, and I wasn't sure which god he thought it was. But I didn't want him to know it was Poseidon.

"What?" Ranger's voice. "What is it?"

The whispers pulled Greg's mutter to me. "Zeus." I heard Ranger's intake of breath even as I exhaled. The whispers were not happy with me in that moment; I could sense their disapproval.

Well, too bad for them. I'm wasn't going to give him another reason to take on my debt. I would need to tell Ranger the truth, though, and Virgil would know by the time we were back. Ranger could tell Maniac. They would need to know which god it was letting his monsters roam our streets. Because, according to the myths and legends and what the whispers were murmuring in my ears, the Minotaurs were his too.

The question was why. And why had he stepped in to stop them this time but not the others?

I let the whispers go, stepping back out of the room, leaving footprints in the hallway. How the monsters managed to get out without leaving trails of blood everywhere was beyond me. Why had they left them in that one room if they didn't leave them anywhere else?

White made an irritated noise. "I'm going to need to get shoe impressions so the idiots down at the precinct don't think we have a suspect."

"No," Greg said. "I'm not giving them anything." He picked me up, stepping us away from the trail I had left. "Ranger?"

Ranger held out a hand, the air twisting, and the footprints disappeared, as if they tracked themselves backwards.

White stared at the now clean wood. "I'm glad he's on our side."

CHAPTER ELEVEN

Ranger took Maniac to go get something to eat while Greg took us back to the Tower

We landed on the balcony, and when we passed back into the living room, I headed straight for the kitchen and the basket left sitting on the island counter. Greg made a strangled noise, trying to catch my arm, but I slid around him.

"Meg—" he started, but I was already there examining it.

There was no card this time. I circled, leaning onto the island so I could view the whole thing without having to move the basket itself. I didn't want to touch it with Greg hovering like that.

"I think it's just here to replace the one that got blown up," I said.

"Why is he so interested in leaving you things?" he said irritated.

"I don't know," I said. "Maybe he really is contrite about the whole compulsion thing."

Greg snorted. "I would prefer he just avoid us entirely in that case." He wrapped an arm around my waist, gently pulling at me where his hand rested on my hip. "We need to go tell Virgil."

"Hmm," I said, letting him lead me out the door and down the stairs to Virgil's apartment, where he knocked on the door.

There was a long pause where I wasn't sure Virgil was home. It was possible he had gone patrolling at some point, but I would think he would've told Greg at least. We rarely left the Tower without texting, calling or verbally telling someone on the team where we would be. Then the locks flipped, and Virgil pulled the door open.

"Greg," he said, his voice sounding thick with sleep. "What happened?"

"Monster attack. They got interrupted by Zeus and then went after Ranger and Maniac in the street."

Virgil's attention sharpened, and he looked at Greg and then me. "Did they now?"

"Yup," I said.

"They're a different type," Greg told him, and Virgil's focus changed, but from the look in his eyes, he wasn't letting this go.

Which was fine. I would need to make sure someone knew the truth, someone who would know when to tell Greg.

"Are Ranger and Maniac okay?" Virgil asked.

"Yes, Ranger took her to get something to eat before they come back here."

Virgil rubbed the bridge of his nose, pulled his phone out, and checked the time. "It's 2:00 am now. Meg, if you need to lie down, I can come sit in the apartment with you. Greg, do you feel up to going back to Royal Park and keeping an ear out?"

"Maniac barbecued the ones that were out," I protested.

"How many?" Virgil asked.

"There were eight," Greg told him.

"How many did you count at the second scene, Meg? Not the second one from tonight, the one where White took over as the lead investigator."

"Five," I grumbled.

"Their numbers are increasing," Virgil said. "We can't count on those eight being the only ones out there."

Greg nodded, gave me a quick kiss, and headed back out and up the stairwell.

Virgil waited a moment, then turned to me. "Which apartment do you want to be in?"

I sighed, turned, and headed to the one down the hallway near the elevator. I opened the door, went into the living room and plopped down on the couch, settling my feet on the coffee table. Virgil followed me, shutting the door behind us, and sat down in the armchair at the end of the table, off to my right. He got himself settled, ankle resting on his knee, fingers steepled as he watched me, waiting.

"I'm not going to know when he's actually left the building," I pointed out.

"Hmm," Virgil said. "You're not. Well, I can tell you, it's safe for you to explain yourself."

"They're Poseidon's monsters," I said, "and Greg told me."

"Told you what?"

"His plan."

"To?"

"Seriously?" I said. "You're going to make me explain it when you, one, already know, and two, can just read my mind anyway?"

"I am."

"Why do you that?" I asked, frustrated.

"I am not infallible. My power is not all-knowing, and discussing it gives me a feel for your motivations."

I rolled my eyes. Virgil, for his part, ignored my attitude, waiting patiently, and as always, his patience outlasted mine. "Greg told me he intended to take on my debt, so when we could sense Poseidon had been there, I didn't tell Greg which god, just that it was a god."

"And let him draw his own conclusions?"

"Yes. I didn't want it to give him more of an excuse to go searching Poseidon out."

Virgil sat there, watching me, his look considering. "He

will be hurt when he finds out you hid this from him."

"I know," I said.

Virgil simply nodded. "You should rest. I'll sit here until Greg returns."

It was a dismissal, so I got up and headed back to our bedroom. It took a long time for me to fall asleep, as the whispers spent the better part of the night murmuring in my ears. The feeling I got from them was that they didn't disagree with my goal, but they did disagree with my methods.

If I was lucky, Greg would never need to know.

∞

When I finally stumbled my way out of our bedroom in the morning – because what sleep I had gotten had been broken by dreams of cribs and red eyes – Greg still wasn't back, and Virgil was dozing, arms crossed, half-tilted to the side in the armchair. He straightened up when I came in, one hand rubbing his eyes.

"Greg hasn't returned," he said, pulling his phone out. "Ranger and Maniac have been back since 3:30."

"What time is it now?" I asked.

"8:00."

I sat down on the couch. "Did you already tell them?"

"No, I let them go rest." He was texting. "Hopefully they're awake and we can handle this before Greg returns." His phone pinged. "Good, they're on their way."

I got up, headed into the kitchen and searched the cabinets for coffee supplies, but found nothing. The fridge, pantry, cabinets and drawers were empty, although plates and utensils were available.

"The empty apartments aren't stocked," Virgil called to me.

"I can see that," I said, when I got back into the living room and sat back down on the couch. "Didn't want to tell me before I went searching?"

159

"No," Virgil said, amusement in his eyes. He gave a careless wave of his hand, and I heard the click of the deadbolt. There was a knock at the front door. "It's open," he called, and Ranger and Maniac came in, pausing for a moment before they picked seats, Ranger in the armchair facing Virgil and Maniac on the couch next to me.

"Meg has a confession to make," Virgil said.

"Why am I telling this story?" I asked, and Virgil shot me a look down his nose, his fingers steepled. I muttered and looked down at the floor. "I let Greg come to the wrong conclusion about which god the monsters belonged to."

"So which one is it?" Maniac asked.

"Poseidon," I said.

"The one you owe," Ranger said flatly. "You lied to him." He pulled out his phone.

"What are you doing?" I asked.

"I'm calling him."

"No," Virgil said. "It cannot come from you. Meg needs to tell him when the time is right."

"How is the time not right now?" Ranger demanded. "I thought we weren't hiding shit from each other."

"He intends to take on Meg's debt himself, and for something we don't know the price of, we can't risk him running off to seek Poseidon out on his own."

"How is that a problem? He's indestructible!" Ranger was shouting at this point. "What could possibly—"

"It could break him," Virgil snapped. "Whatever task Poseidon sets that he has to fulfill, he could slide somewhere he cannot go again."

"So it's okay to not break him, but we're just going to let Meg shatter instead?" Ranger asked snidely.

"Would you take her place?" Virgil asked.

"Yes," Ranger said, with no hesitation.

"Meg, would you let any of us transfer the debt to ourselves?" Virgil asked.

"No," I said.

Virgil motioned at me. "There you have it. This is Meg's choice."

"That's—" Ranger started. "You didn't see her when she got back, she—" he seemed to be struggling to find the words.

"I did not," Virgil said quietly, "but circumstances have changed, and we can only hope that Hera's blessing will discourage Poseidon from making any kind of request that would cause Meg permanent harm."

"I think you're putting all your eggs in one basket, when you have other solutions readily available," Ranger said.

Virgil held up a hand. "I understand your viewpoint, but we will need to table this discussion—"

"I'm not tabling this!" Ranger was shouting again, Maniac trying to shush him when the front door opened.

Greg came into the living room, carrying a drinks tray with two lidded cups and a paper bag from the coffee shop back by our old temporary headquarters. Stiffly, he set both down on the coffee table in front of the rest of us, and then stepped back, crossing his arms. "Table what discussion?"

"Meg and Virgil are hiding shit again," Ranger said.

"Everyone out," Greg said quietly.

Ranger's face had taken on a surprised, then mulish expression. "No."

"Everyone out but Meg," Greg said.

"No," Virgil said.

"I am not having this discussion in front of an audience," Greg said. "Meg and I will talk about things that affect our relationship without the rest of you and your interjections."

"I'm afraid you'll have to include me on this discussion," Virgil said. "Because it's my fault that she hid it from you to begin with."

"If you're all going to start shouting, I'm sitting right here," Maniac said.

Greg scrubbed at his face. "Just fucking explain."

"It wasn't Zeus who was at the scene. It was Poseidon. The ones showing up are his monsters," I said, eyes on the floor.

"You—" Greg started, then stopped. "God damn it, Meg." He had a hand in his hair. "You can't hide this shit from me!"

"I'm sorry," I said.

"Then stop doing it!"

The whispers were smug in my ears, and I waved them off, blinking tears out of my eyes.

"You can't place all the blame—" Virgil said.

"I know exactly who to place the blame on!" Greg shouted. "She ignores any advice, no matter who gives it to her. Don't act like what you say bears further weight!"

"She places exactly the right amount of weight to anything I tell her when it pertains to you," Virgil said calmly. "She does, in fact, ignore me on all other matters. And if you would stop and think, you would realize she is, albeit frustratingly for you, trying to protect you."

"She doesn't need to protect me! I can—"

"Rescue yourself?" Virgil asked.

"That is not the same, and you know it," Greg said.

I desperately wanted to tell them I was sitting right here, but didn't want to attract anyone's attention at the same time.

Maniac did it for me. "You know she's sitting right here, right?"

I snorted, and that made Greg glare at me. "This isn't funny," he said. "Don't lie to me."

I opened my mouth to protest that technically I hadn't lied, and he pointed a finger at me. "No, I know what you're going to say, and it's still a lie."

I shut my mouth and looked back down the floor, my face burning.

Ranger was being silent.

"Are you happy now?" I shot at him.

"Yes," he said. "We're a team, we don't hide things.

You lied to all of us."

"Fine," I said and got up from the couch.

"You don't get to be the one storming off," Ranger said.

"Watch me," I snapped, moving past Virgil in his armchair, headed out of the living room.

"Meg," Greg said, and it was the way he said my name that made me stop and turn to look at him. "Meg, please. Let me be what I am."

Guardian, said the whispers. A vague insistence that they were heroes created and meant to stand between the gods and their machinations.

I've never put much store in fate.

But all I said was, "Okay."

"Okay?" he asked.

"Okay," I said, and I left the room, headed for our bedroom.

∞

I wasn't in there pouting for long before Greg followed me. He was carrying one of the cups from the drinks tray he had brought in with him and something wrapped in paper. He set both down on the bedside table and then sat on the bed next to me, wrapping an arm over my shoulders and pulling me against him. I relaxed into him, because while I didn't deserve it in the moment, I needed the comfort.

"Do you know why?" he asked me quietly.

"No," I said. "I don't know what he's after letting them into the city."

"Will he be angry at you or us for killing them?"

"I don't know."

Greg sighed, then nodded. "Don't go anywhere with him."

I straightened up, mouth opened to protest.

"Meg, I know you."

He did. If Greg was at risk, I would throw caution to

the wind and go with Poseidon to keep Greg safe.

He pulled me back against him, put his nose in my hair and kissed my head. "I'm still mad at both you and Virgil for lying to me about this."

I relaxed into his side again. "You don't feel mad," I said cautiously. Because he didn't; he wasn't tense beneath me.

He snagged the paper-wrapped object off the table and held it out in front of me. "I got you breakfast."

I took it, but didn't unwrap it, just sat holding it. "Did you find any more of those things last night?"

"No." Gently he put his hands over mine, pulling the paper back. "You need to eat."

I shook my head, trying to pull my hands free so I could set the sandwich down. Just the smell of it was making me feel sick.

"Meg," he sounded exasperated.

"I'm not trying to be difficult!" I said, my stomach rolling. "I can't eat it." He plucked the sandwich from my hands and set it down on the table, shifting with me as I moved forward, kneeling on hands and knees. His hand was on my back, his face by mine as he leaned over.

I was trying not to vomit or cry, and I couldn't keep both back at the same time. Greg put his free hand on my face and was brushing tears away with his fingers.

"Breathe, Meg."

"I can't do this," I said.

His hand stilled; I could feel the flexing of his fingers on my back. "Do what?"

I waved a hand helplessly, trying to encompass the feeling that I was drowning in. "This. The – I didn't sign up for gods," was all I managed, lamely.

"We could leave."

I shook my head. "I can't do that, either."

"Meg, you're pregnant. No one would blame you for retiring."

"That's not the problem. I can't—" I was frustrated

because I couldn't figure out how to explain the growing feeling of dread sitting on my chest, and leaving wouldn't alleviate it. The gods would find me anyway.

I sat back because the sick feeling had passed, and now he pulled me back against him, his arms wrapped around me. "Everyone is still in the living room. Do you want me to tell them to go?"

"Whose shift is it?"

"Ranger's."

Damn it. "Yes."

"You just don't want to sit with Ranger because he's mad at you."

"No," I muttered. "It's because he'll want to talk out our feelings."

Greg snorted and started chuckling, his ribs rumbling against mine. After a moment, he sobered. "I think you should talk out your feelings. You can't just let these things build up."

"I don't want therapy."

"Meg—" he sighed.

"Who do you talk to?" I interrupted before he could badger me.

"Virgil," he said simply.

"Do you talk to Virgil about me?"

"Yes," he admitted.

"About?" and I couldn't keep the irritation from coloring my tone.

He was silent for a long moment, and I wasn't sure he would answer me. "I'm scared," he said finally. "I'm afraid that I won't be able to keep the two of you safe."

I didn't know what to say to that. I had no way to reassure him, and when I didn't answer him, he tightened his arms and switched subjects. "We've also still got dinner with my family tonight."

"Fuck. Where? What time?"

"Some Italian place, *Bella Notte*, and around 6:00. My mom made reservations."

"Do we have to dress up?"

"It's casual."

"How casual? Because I think your casual and my casual are two very different things."

"Family style dinner casual."

"That answers nothing," I said. "Am I going to get us kicked out if I'm in jeans?"

"Won't matter," Virgil said from the doorway, looking at something on his phone. "The new suit is in. I'm going down to the street to get our delivery. You will need to wear clothing that hides it when you go out. That means long sleeves and pants."

He disappeared from view, and Greg yelled after him, "Timing!"

"That was good timing," I said. "It was actually relevant."

"Don't tell him that, or he'll find excuses to do it more often." Greg was loosening his arms, scooting us back up the bed. "Lie back."

"Why?" I asked, doing it anyway, and he settled with his head on my stomach, one hand on one of my thighs.

"Because I flew around for six hours last night. And you sound like you didn't sleep."

"Not well," I admitted.

"So, take a nap," he said. "I've got you."

I lay my head down, one hand resting on his back, one in his hair, and closed my eyes.

But I didn't sleep. Instead, my thoughts chased themselves around. Were Guardians what they were because they were fated to be one from the start, or did that become their fate once they loved a god?

What had made Greg mine, and when?

The whispers were no help because as far as they were concerned, Hera's Guardian had always been with her.

Some bang up job he did.

Eventually I gave up on sleep, sliding out from under

Greg by telling him I needed to figure out something to eat. He had woken up enough to ask if I needed him to go with me, and I had told him if Ranger wasn't in the apartment, I would come back and get him.

I did mean it. If he had heard a lie, he would've gotten up immediately, but he settled his head down and went back to sleep.

Ranger was in the living room when I went to go check, sitting in the same armchair, and he looked up from his phone when I stepped into the doorway.

"You over yourself?" he asked.

"Yes," I said.

He waited, watching me.

"What?" I asked.

"You going to apologize?"

"For what?" I asked, just to be difficult, but at the expression he made, the frustrated, hurt look he had, I groaned. "I'm sorry. Don't make me talk out my feelings again."

He smirked at me.

"I didn't intend to lie to you," I said. "I was going to wait until Greg was busy and tell you the truth to make sure someone knew. In case—" I stopped because I realized I had responded to that smirk automatically, so I glared at him.

"We're a team," Ranger said. "We need to be making decisions about how to handle this stuff together. Don't hide evidence from us."

"Thought we were a family," I said, flopping down on the couch and putting my feet up.

Ranger looked like he was about to respond to that, but my stomach chose that minute to rumble. I transferred my glare to it. Oh, sure, now it's hungry.

"You haven't eaten?" he asked.

"No," I said.

"Greg brought you a sandwich."

I looked away from him. "I couldn't eat it."

"What was wrong with it?"

"I don't know. I just couldn't – it just didn't smell right."

Ranger looked like he was thinking, then he got up. "Come on. We're going to get you something to eat."

I got up from the couch. "I don't know that you're going to fare any better than Greg has with finding things I can stomach."

"Oh, ye of little faith," Ranger said, taking a quick trip down the hallway to knock on the bedroom door frame. "I'm taking Meg out to figure out what she can eat."

Greg's reply was too mumbled for me to make it from the living room door, but Ranger chuckled and come back up the hallway to me.

"What?" I asked as we went out the front door. "What did he say?"

"Good luck."

We headed into the elevator, and Ranger hit the button for street level. "We're not going on the bike?" I asked him.

"Nah, place I'm thinking of is right up the street."

"What place?"

"Fro-yo."

"Fro-yo," I said slowly.

"Yeah, frozen yogurt."

"I know what fro-yo is. That—" I had to pause, because on second thought, it sounded mildly healthy at least. Yogurt is good for you, right? The thought made me pause, because nutrition content used to be my least concern when it came to food. Greg and Virgil's food preferences were rubbing off on me, and I couldn't decide if this was an improvement.

When the elevator doors opened, we were trying to step out at the same time Virgil was stepping on. Virgil sighed. "Where are you going?"

"For fro-yo," Ranger told him. "Meg hasn't eaten. Want us to bring you some back?"

"No, thank you," Virgil said. He had a garment box tucked under one arm. "Try not to take long."

We traded spots, the elevator doors closing behind us, and Ranger led me outside to the street, and down to our right on the sidewalk. There were a ton of people out, and he caught my arm, his hand on my elbow, as he pulled me next to him. He left his hand there, his fingers curled around my arm.

"Don't want to lose you," he said.

"I think I'd be able to find my way back to the Tower."

"I'd never hear the end of it from attack dog if I lost you on a sidewalk," he said, choosing to follow my lead and gloss by what I heard in his voice.

"How far is it?"

"Couple blocks up and half of one over."

We walked in silence. Well, we stopped talking. A city like this is never silent. There were cars coming up and down the street, the chatter of the pedestrians walking in groups, the clicking footfalls of the ones alone headed to various business meetings. I could hear someone shouting, whistling for a cab. A guy went whizzing by on a skateboard, almost knocking into Ranger, who dodged to the side into me, his free hand catching at my waist to make sure he didn't knock me down in his quest to get out of the way.

"Jesus, some people," he muttered, letting go and stepping back.

"This isn't even rush hour," I said. "It gets worse."

He towed me forward again, turning us down the corner, grinning at me. "You act like I've never lived in a city before."

"You're the one who knows all about bears."

"I did not grow up in the wilderness. Whatever impression you got."

"You told me you moved around a lot. How do I know you didn't?"

"It involved a lot of cheap motels. Here," he pulled me toward the door, swinging it open out of the way and waiting for me to go first.

"Are there monsters?"

"There's gummy bears."

"Are they monstrous gummy bears?" I asked, heading into the store.

"They're pretty toothless, so I think you can take them," he said following me. The door swung shut behind us.

This was the first time I'd ever been in a fro-yo shop, and curiously I looked around. The store was mostly empty, only a few people loitering at the metal tables and chairs, the kind that would be better on an outdoor patio. They were going to scratch the shit out of the tile flooring. The checkout counter was by the door, and all along the interior walls were dispensers, flavor labels hung over each one. At the end between the dispensers and the counter was a toppings bar. Not only were there a ridiculous number of candies to choose from, including the aforementioned gummy bears, there were slices of fresh fruit, your typical ones like strawberries, bananas, kiwi, and then fruits I had never had before, like dragon fruit.

"Pick your poison," Ranger said, motioning at all the different flavors.

I had no idea where to start.

Look, I'm indecisive at the best of times. Don't put this kind of pressure on me.

Ranger sighed. "Okay, fine, you're going to make me do it." He steered me over to a table, sat me down and went over to the dispensers. I watched him grab a large bowl and make his way around the various stations before paying at the checkout counter. He came back over to the table with the bowl and a spoon, set them down in front of me and then sat across from me.

"Breakfast is served."

I looked at it. He had topped the yogurt with strawberries, blueberries, and for good measure, gummy bears. "I feel like this is more like brunch."

He snorted. "Just try to eat something. Attack dog is going to have a fit if you fade away from starvation."

Well, it didn't smell like much, so I picked up the spoon and tentatively tried some. When my stomach didn't protest, I ended up devouring it. I was scraping the bowl when Ranger pulled out his phone and started texting someone.

"What are you doing?" I asked.

"Telling Greg to stock you up on foods you can eat cold," he said.

I thought about it. Come to think of it, he was right. Everything that had made my stomach roll over recently had been food meant to be eaten hot. Guess I wasn't eating anything at dinner with Greg's family tonight. Ranger was still texting though. "Now who are you messaging?"

"Maniac, to see if she wants us to bring her some back."

"What about Greg?"

"He already said no."

It left me at a loss for the conversation. Ranger had already demonstrated consideration I hadn't expected from him, with the whole give a gift to Greg meant for me thing. I suppose I shouldn't have been surprised he would do it for small things, too.

He looked up from his phone, then looked at me. "What?"

I shrugged.

"You can't give me that look and not explain it."

"Would you really take on the debt?"

"Yes. It's what family does."

I was silent, staring at my empty bowl.

"Why don't you talk to your parents?" Ranger asked.

I looked up, focusing on his eyes. "How come you never talk about yours?"

"My mom died from cancer a few years ago."

"Oh," I said. "I'm sorry." I focused back on the table. "What about your dad?"

"Heard he got hit by a train. Couldn't have happened to someone more deserving." There was a venom to his voice I had never heard before, and that made me look back up. The hard look on his face answered a question I hadn't wanted to ask.

"We're all just different shades of fucked up?" I asked instead.

"Greg's family seems normal," Ranger said, relaxing back against his chair.

"I feel like there's a lot of tension in it. They don't get him."

"Because he went from grand theft auto to a man of the law? I feel like a lot of cops get their start that way."

I snorted. "No. Well, maybe. From what Brit's told me, his mom spoiled him rotten. But that's coming from Tony, so who knows."

"Sounds like typical baby of the family kind of stuff to me," Ranger said. "You haven't answered my question though."

"Which one?" I asked, pretending ignorance.

He snorted this time. "Don't be like that. Why don't you talk to your parents?"

"We just don't have a relationship."

"Yeah, I get that. But something had to happen to end the relationship to start with."

"Are we doing the find out what makes someone tick thing again?"

"You're practicing avoidance."

"You know, Greg hasn't even asked me this question."

"I'm not Greg."

I scowled at him.

"You know I'm not going to let this go. I'll just repeat it until you get pissed off enough to yell the answer at me."

I looked back down at my bowl. "They kicked me out when I was eighteen."

"Lots of kids get told to figure out their shit at eighteen," Ranger said. "What made them telling you to move out any different?"

"Because they gave up on me two years before that," I snapped. "They got home and couldn't even go into our house because of me. They had to come get me from a facility;

nobody knew what to do with me. The doctors didn't know what to do, the nurses were afraid of me, and the fucking general they sent to talk to me about hero work took one look at me and ran. My parents wouldn't speak to me, they wouldn't touch me, they could barely look at me."

He was silent, watching me. "You haven't told Greg any of this?"

"He read my file; he probably already knows."

"I feel like it's different, getting it from the viewpoint of the source."

I stood up. "Well, I don't want to talk about it."

He got up with me. "You're not your parents."

I gaped at him, closed my mouth, and glared at him. "Okay, Virgil." I headed for the door, and he caught up to me.

"You know, some of us don't need to be psychic to be insightful."

We were outside on the sidewalk, him keeping pace with me as I went back toward the Tower. "Could you not?" I said.

"No," he said. "If you can't talk to attack dog about the things that scare you, who can you talk to? Virgil? You're not going to express it because you're just going to assume he already knows."

"I don't need a therapist."

"I think you're wrong there."

"Oh my God," I said stopping to face him. "Does every conversation with you have to be like this? Can't we have one that just stays surface level?"

"All your conversations would be surface level."

"They would not," I said, flaring up. "I talk to Greg, just not about this."

He was looking down at me. "Why not?"

"I don't want to!" I shouted at him. I could feel the whispers tug at me, the scent of myrtles and roses in the air. Someone laughed, a sound like tinkling bells, and the whispers tugged again, murmuring, but I was too busy yelling at Ranger to listen to them. "Jesus Christ, some people actually respect that there are subjects people want to keep to themselves!"

He kissed me.

I jerked away, hauled back and slapped him.

He stood there, looking just as surprised as I felt, one hand on his face. "Shit."

"What is wrong with you?!" I yelled at him, my palm and fingers stinging.

"I'm sorry, Meg, I don't know what—" he was stammering.

I turned, stomping up the street, and he caught up to me, still apologizing. "Meg, Meg, wait! I wasn't, I didn't mean to—"

"I don't care."

"Jesus, would you just listen?" he yelled at me.

I stopped, turning to face him. "I already listened," I pointed out, "and then you kissed me. I'm going to pretend it didn't happen."

He looked just as surprised by that as he was by the fact that he had kissed me in the middle of the street. "You're not going to tell attack dog to stomp me into the curb?"

"I don't need his help with that."

"No, you don't," he admitted. "You can't lie to him about this to protect me."

"He's going to know even if I don't say anything," I said. "Because I'm going to be hella awkward and avoiding you as much as possible for the next week at least."

"He's going to punch me, isn't he?"

"Probably."

"I would fuck this up," Ranger muttered.

I shrugged and started up the sidewalk again. Ranger followed me, his hands in his pockets, brooding the rest of the way to the Tower.

CHAPTER TWELVE

Greg wasn't in the apartment when we got back, so now I had a choice: run and hide with Virgil, hide in our bedroom, or sit on the couch pretending nothing had happened.

I curled up in a corner of the couch, pressed into the cushions as much as I could be.

Ranger chose the armchair as far from me as possible. He was still brooding.

I looked around for the remote for the TV but didn't see one on any of the available surfaces, and the silence was making me itch.

"What are you going to tell Maniac?"

"The truth," Ranger said.

"She going to be mad at you?"

"Probably." He was fidgeting and ended up leaning forward with his elbows on his knees, fingers interlocked as he looked at me. "Thought you were going to avoid me?"

I looked at the floor. "If I hide now, Greg's going to think I'm hiding from him."

Ranger nodded, that brooding look back on his face.

The front door opened and closed. Greg came in carrying one of the reusable grocery bags he keeps stocked under the kitchen sink, and it looked very full. He took one look at Ranger's face and swore. "God damn it."

He went into the kitchen, came back out without the bag, and looked at me. "Meg, would you mind putting the groceries in the fridge? I need to talk to Ranger."

I hesitated for a moment and then hopped off the couch and headed into the kitchen.

Yes, I was weighing how well I would be able to eavesdrop. What did you think I was doing?

Very quietly, I started unloading things from the bag. It was all things that could be eaten cold, other than the carton of eggs. There was produce – for Greg's salads – but also lots of yogurt and fruits for me. I smiled at the container of whole milk, plain Greek yogurt. Poor Greg. It must have been the only one that fit his no sugar rule, and he had to choose between that and not making me pull a me and toss it just because it's Greek.

There was a bottle of honey from a local farm. Well, in state, which is as local as you could get since the farms are miles outside the city. I thought about it for a moment: maybe Virgil would want to put a beehive up on the roof. He could make sure he didn't get stung without needing smoke or the special suit.

I was still straining my ears, listening, but no one was saying anything yet. I opened the fridge door and purposely rustled the bag.

That was when I heard Greg's voice. "What happened?"

Ranger's response was too quiet for me to make out; he was muttering again.

"You what?" Greg's voice had darkened.

Ranger repeated what he had said, irritation coloring his words this time, because he knew Greg had heard exactly what he said. "I kissed Meg. She slapped me, so don't get mad at her."

I paused in my picking up of the lettuce, because it had gone silent again, and I was debating if I should sneak over to the door to peek out.

I heard Greg sigh, "Meg."

I turned and started haphazardly loading things into the fridge. There was no sense or order to where I was putting the food, but I was making enough noise that Greg must have felt it covered their discussion enough.

"Why," and his tone was harsh, "the fuck would you do that?"

"You're not going to just hit me?" Ranger asked.

"I haven't decided," Greg said. "Apparently Meg already made her feelings on it clear. Answer the question."

"I don't know. She was yelling at me about how she didn't want to talk about her parents, and—" he paused, I heard the intake of breath like he was going to start again, but there was only silence for a long moment. "Could you just hit me? The suspense is the worst part."

"Let him sit in suspense!" I yelled from the kitchen.

Greg chuckled, and that surprised me. He cut the laugh short though. "Meg, groceries. Stop eavesdropping." I could still hear the amusement in his voice.

I had all the groceries in, and if I stood here pretending to put away more, I was going to waste all the cold air. I shut the fridge door.

He had gotten coffee and filters, so I found the grinder and got started on making a pot because I still hadn't had any this morning. I had sort of dozed with Greg and had left the cup he had brought me, forgotten on the bedside table.

I snuck over to stand by the kitchen door so I could hear what they were saying over the noise the grinder made. I peeked out.

Greg was still standing, his arms crossed. He was looming over Ranger, who was still sitting, elbows on his knees, head hanging. Greg's looming didn't look intentional, but it was hard to tell since his back was to me. I saw Greg scrub at his face.

"What did she tell you about her parents?"

"I'm not – you can ask her about it," Ranger said. "She said she hadn't told you and I'm not going to circumvent her like that."

Greg made an irritated noise. "But you'll kiss her."

"I didn't mean for it to happen! I don't even—" Ranger stopped there, because he had looked up to yell at Greg in the first place, and now he spotted me peering around the doorframe. I ducked back. "I don't even know why I did it," Ranger finished. "I can't explain what I was thinking." He was silent again. "Why aren't you just punching me?"

"If you want me to hit you that badly I can," Greg said, "but Meg already defended herself."

"I feel like you should be angrier than you are," Ranger said, sounding cautious.

Greg sounded frustrated. "I can hear the truth in what you're saying. I know how you feel about her." Ranger started to protest, and Greg cut him off. "No, I know. Virgil knows. The only one who doesn't seem to know is Maniac. I'm not worried about that, but what I am worried about is if you acted on your own or if there's another god out there influencing people."

"I thought their compulsions couldn't affect me," Ranger said, "and I'm not going to take that olive branch just so I can weasel my way out of my own actions."

"We know Meg and Bacchus can't affect you. There's at least—" Greg paused. "Meg, how many have we not tested?"

"Two," I said, poking my head back around the door.

"Two," Greg said, turning back to Ranger. "Two we can't confirm. I know what Virgil's theory is, and I know that I'm willing to trust it. But we don't know – everything we have in the tales could be wrong. I'm willing to extend you the grace that there may have been outside forces at work in that moment."

"And if not?" Ranger asked.

"I'll punch you later when we're done dealing with man eaters."

Ranger grinned at him. "What, like brothers?"

Greg snorted. "You don't want me to punch you as

hard as I would punch one of them."

"That puts a hole in Virgil's 'no gods around me when you guys are here' theory," I pointed out.

"Did any of them come talk to you?" Greg asked. "Call you to them?"

"No," I said.

"Them not coming up to you directly might be all we can hope for. If they were there, they may have been hoping you would leave Ranger behind so they could approach you then."

I paused and thought about it. "Damn it," I said because it wasn't an unreasonable thought. I switched topics. Sort of. "Is Maniac going to set you on fire?"

"No. She might dump me though," Ranger said.

"I am running upstairs to retrieve Meg's sodas. Don't do anything," Greg said, and he headed out the front door.

Ranger looked at me when we heard the stairwell door close. "Is he lying to himself just so he can justify not hitting me?"

I came out of the kitchen and sat down on the armchair since it left more space between us. "I don't think so. What he's saying isn't out of the realm of possibilities, and there's at least one monster in addition to the two gods we can't test Virgil's theory with."

"I'm always surprised when he thinks things through."

"Why?" I said, my tone nastier than I had intended. "He's not an idiot."

"Not because of that," Ranger said. "He tends to be angry a lot. He just seems like the type to hit first and ask questions later."

"I was," Greg said, startling both of us when he came back in. "Virgil helped a lot with that." He passed by carrying the open pack of root beers into the kitchen. I heard the fridge door open, the clunk of the cans as he set them down, and the door closing. He came back out and set a root beer on the coffee table in front of me. "You forgot to start the coffee pot." He knelt next to me, one hand on my knee.

"When did you meet Virgil?" I asked.

"About seven or eight years ago. I had already been contracted for at least a couple years before they stationed me here."

"Where did they have you before?" Ranger asked.

"Area 51."

"That doesn't exist," I said.

"Oh, it does. It's where they take any heroes who enlist for training."

"They had you in training for two years?" Ranger asked.

"No, they just had me stationed there for two years."

"Why?" I asked.

Greg shrugged. "Never asked."

"How'd you end up meeting Virgil?"

"He hit me with a car," Greg said.

"Wait, Virgil's wrecked more than once?" Ranger asked. "I'm never letting him live this down."

"Why do all your first times meeting other heroes involve you guys hitting each other?" I asked.

"You didn't hit me," he said.

"Wasn't a hero at the time," I pointed out.

"Yes, you were, you just didn't know it yet." He was smiling at me, warmth in his eyes.

"On that note, I'm out," Ranger said. "Unless you want me to finish my shift."

"I think I've got it covered," Greg said.

"Right," Ranger said, and he got up from the chair. I heard the front door close behind him.

Greg got up and left the living room. There was the click of the deadbolt flipping; then he came back and leaned over me. I tilted my head up so now his lips were hovering over mine. He kissed me, one hand on my face. He pulled back, scooped me up off the armchair, and set me on my feet. He hugged me to him, his nose in my hair.

"Do you think it was a god?" he asked me.

"I don't know," I said honestly. I had been too focused on yelling at Ranger in the first place to pay attention to who was around us.

Greg sighed, his breath stirring my curls. "I like him," he grumbled. "I don't want to have to punch him."

"So don't," I said. "Let him wait in 'am I getting punched?' limbo."

Greg chuckled, his arms tightening briefly, and he put a hand back on my face, his thumb brushing my cheek. "We've got a while before we have to go meet everyone for dinner."

"Guess we'll need to find something to do."

He kissed me, his free hand sliding up my shirt, the hand on my face in my hair now. I responded, my own hands slipping up his shirt, my fingers brushing along his skin, but then he stopped, pulling back.

"Are you tickling me?" he asked.

"Maybe," I said.

"That's not going to work," he said, his voice husky as he bent back over me. I tried to move back from him, but he had a hand on my waist, the fingers of his free hand skimming along my ribs. I laughed, and tried again to squirm away, but he had me fast, and then he bodily lifted me up, his lips on mine again, and he was carrying me to the bedroom.

For a moment, I thought I could smell myrtle and roses, but it was there and then gone, and I couldn't be sure the scent had existed at all.

∞

Tony, Peter, Brit and Sandra didn't bring the kids to dinner. Sandra told me they were viewing it as a rare date night since they don't go out often. Even though Greg's mom had made reservations, we all had to awkwardly stand around for a moment while they made sure our table was ready.

When the hostess finally came back to lead us to where we were going to be seated, Greg put his hand on the small of my back. He had hesitated for a minute when we reached our table because he was trying to judge where the safest spot to put me was, but our table was in the middle of the restaurant, and his choice was either our backs to the kitchen, or our backs to the entrance, and any of the diners in between the two.

Tony ended up making the choice for him when he seated Brit with their backs to the front windows, so Greg led us around to the other side, sticking me in one of the middle seats. Sandra ended up next to me, Peter and Greg flanking the ends, and their mother was across from me.

I'm pretty sure she chose that seat on purpose because now she was staring me down.

There awkward silence continued while the waitress got drink orders, told us the specials and left us with the menus. Looking it over, I realized we were all going to have to come to a compromise on what went on the table because Greg was serious about the restaurant serving family style dinners.

I took a moment to look around. All the tables had those red and white checkered style tablecloths that are ubiquitous to Italian restaurants everywhere, the wine bottles with the skinny half-melted candle placed in the mouth.

"What about the veal?" Tony asked, looking at the menu. I saw Brit roll her eyes.

"Some people can't eat that," she said pointedly.

"We can order more than one dish," he said, sounding snappish.

"It's fine," Greg said. "I think I can handle having just pasta if no one wants the eggplant." He looked over at Brit. "Not everything he does is to get under my skin."

She blinked at him and patted Tony's hand. "Sorry, honey."

"It's fine," he grunted.

"I like eggplant," Sandra said.

"Veal and eggplant, sounds good," Peter said, setting down his menu. "So, what's the news this time?"

Greg took a breath. "Meg and I got married. None of

you were invited. Also, she's pregnant."

That was definitely ripping off the band-aid.

The sound of the chatter surrounding us seemed incredibly loud compared to the silence at the table and the stunned looks on their mother's and Tony's faces.

"Still throwing you a wedding party," Brit said. She thought about it for a second. "Maybe we should just make it a combo wedding and baby shower. Can you wear a wedding dress to a baby shower?"

"I don't see why not. It's her – excuse me – their baby," Sandra said.

"For the sake of not giving the reporters any fodder, can we please keep the two events separate?" Greg said. "Or just not do them at all?"

"You can't not have a baby shower!" Sandra said.

"I think we absolutely can not have a baby shower," I said.

"Oh no, you have to have one," Brit said, Sandra nodding along with her.

"Can we—" I started but the waitress was back, setting down drinks in front of us before taking our order and heading back off.

"When are you due?" Greg's mother asked.

"April 27th," Greg said.

"Little early to be telling people, isn't it?" Tony asked.

"Technically," Greg said, "but the news already figured it out, and we had to tell Vigilante and the rest of the team anyway."

"Are you going to be retiring? Either of you?" Tony asked.

"No," I said. Greg's hand had made its way to my knee, and I felt his fingers flex, his thumb brushing back and forth.

"No?" he asked me, half teasing.

"No," I said. "We'll get Auntie Maniac to babysit when we go out."

Greg laughed, a sputter to it. "Auntie Maniac?"

"She'll love it."

"You're going to leave my grandbaby with someone named Maniac?" Greg's mother said.

"Yes," I said.

"What about when it's your whole team?" Peter asked. "What are you going to do then?"

"We have someone for that," I said.

"Who?" Greg asked me.

"Barbara."

He smiled at me. "I think that would work. I'll ask Vigilante to talk to her, see if she can help when she's not at her diner."

"Bet you he already did."

"I'm sure—" he started, but his phone started ringing. He pulled it out and frowned.

"What?" I said.

"It's Poltergeist, but they shouldn't be back in town already."

"So, answer it?"

He did. "Poltergeist, what—" he didn't finish what he was about to ask, because the look on his face changed from a frown to one of serious concern, "Slow down, I can't—" and then I saw the fear on his face. "What? Did your client say why? How long has it been—" He was standing up, pulling at my arm, "No, no, Vengeance and I are going to be on the move. Call me when—" He dropped the phone as his head shot up, looking away from me, out the front windows. "Shit, everyone get down!" he bellowed.

He jerked the table up, drinks flying, tossing it over people's heads so that it hit the windows. Glass shattered outward, and he snatched me up, following the table's path, twisting so we were headed upward, away from other people, his back to the street, and the van with the open sliding door parked across from the restaurant.

There was a sudden explosive rat-ta-ta-ta-ta, and I could hear the thumping impacts as whatever was being fired at us hit

Greg. He grunted, shooting us straight up. There was a clattering noise as the brick and masonry of the front of the building shattered and he outdistanced them before they could change their aim. He landed on the top, ducking us down behind the parapet, and he peered over.

"Fuck," he said. "I need you to – damn it, they're running. Meg, stay here, I need to—" He stopped because I was shaking, trembling against him. "Meg, look at me. Did they hit you?" He was searching me over.

"Don't leave," I said, because all I could think was that I would be alone in that moment, and if I was lucky, the only one who would show up would be Bacchus.

He swore again, pulling me back against him, my head pressed against his chest. "We need to make sure everyone else is okay." He scrubbed at his face. "And make sure I didn't just break another phone."

"What was the call about?" I asked, trying to focus on anything but my hammering heart.

"Poltergeist said their client offered them another contract, for you."

"Me?" I squeaked. "Why me?"

"They didn't say."

"What did they say?" I demanded. "Are they taking it?"

"No, and they were taking a risk calling me because they hadn't even gotten out of the building."

"Guess they must really like you."

"Where's your phone? We need to tell Virgil."

I pulled it out of my pocket and handed it over.

"Virgil," Greg said when he answered. "Poltergeist's client put out a contract on Meg. Find out who's taken it. Poltergeist refused it, but someone else didn't."

∞

Everyone in the restaurant was shaken but okay. There was some minor property damage other than the windows and table Greg had broken, because when he had blasted us out and up, the machine gun the mercenary or mercenaries in the van across the street had been using had taken out part of the front and some light fixtures.

The police were going door to door on the lower apartments where any of the bullets had hit checking to make sure none of the residents had gotten hurt. Greg's path had taken us between windows so hopefully there was masonry, studs, drywall, furniture and other things in the way of tenants.

His phone had not survived the drop to the floor.

He picked it up, examining the shattered screen.

"Maybe we should start using otter boxes or something," I said.

He scrubbed his face. "I break those too."

"How are you going to manage to raise a child in this environment?" Tony demanded. "You're going to have to retire. What are you going to do when you have to take the baby out? You can't be risking other people's kids just so you can take yours to the park or the beach."

I saw Greg's fingers tighten on his phone and heard the crunching of the glass and metal. I didn't want to admit it, but right now, Tony had a point.

Although we wouldn't take him to the beach anyway.

"I tried to tell you I couldn't live a normal life," Greg said quietly as he slipped the broken phone into his pocket. His head came up; he was looking out the shattered windows, and he sighed. "KBC is here. Meg?" He held out an arm, and I stepped into him so he could pick me up. He turned back to his family. "I'm sorry about dinner."

The crew from the news van was still unloading, and when they saw him come out they started scrambling, but they were too late, because he took off.

CHAPTER THIRTEEN

He landed on our balcony, opened the door, poked his head in and listened before he let me follow him inside. We paused by the couch as he knelt, his ear pressed to my stomach.

I put my hand in his hair and felt his fingers tighten against me.

After a moment, he got up, and we headed out the front door down to Virgil's floor and down to the end of the hall where Virgil's apartment was.

"In here!" Virgil called out from security.

He was on his phone, texting.

"Hear anything?" Greg asked.

"My contact has confirmed there's a contract out on Meg, but the why behind what it's for is unknown."

"For how much?" Greg asked.

"Why does that matter?" I asked. It's bad enough someone is paying people to kill me in the first place.

"Because it will tell us how badly they want you dead," Virgil said. "Along with a rough estimate of how many mercenaries we're going to be fending off. It's one, by the way."

"Someone tried to take out a restaurant full of people for a hundred thousand dollars?" I asked, incensed. What is wrong with people?

"One million," Virgil corrected.

For a moment I was smug that I was worth twice what Mirage was, and then common sense caught up.

What? Sometimes I use it.

I felt the blood drain from my face. "What does that mean?" I asked panicked. Greg pulled me against him, and I could hear his heart under my ear, steady, as constant as he was.

"It means," Virgil said, "that we will need to take out Poltergeist's client much sooner than initially intended. Without someone to pay it, the contract goes away."

Greg pulled what was left of his phone out and held it out to Virgil. "I dropped it."

Virgil examined it. "These indentations aren't usually caused by a drop."

"The drop happened first," I said.

Virgil simply went over to a cabinet, pulled out a box, and opened it up. The two of us stood there, watching him get Greg's new phone activated and set up. Then he handed it over and pulled his own phone back out. "We should have Ranger and Maniac come up so we can explain to them the new development."

Greg cleared his throat, and Virgil shot him a look.

"Ranger kissed me," I said by way of explanation.

Virgil looked surprised. "When?"

"How did you not know that already?" I asked.

"I would also like to know that," Virgil said sharply. "When?"

"This morning, on the way back from getting fro-yo."

"Were there any gods around?"

"I don't know," I said honestly.

Virgil had his hand at his chin. "Ranger is not immune to my ability to influence."

The subject change confused me for a moment, but Greg was faster than I was. "You think one of the gods might be working by influence and not outright compulsion?"

"Yes," Virgil said.

"I thought they were the same thing," I said.

"Influence is more a suggestion, compulsion a command," Virgil said. "At least, that is the best way for me to explain the difference in degree of power. People could choose to ignore my influence; they rarely do because it generally follows the path of least resistance. They cannot ignore your compulsion."

Footsteps sounded down the hallway, and then Maniac and Ranger came in. Maniac marched over to stand next to me, leaving Ranger back by the door.

"Heard you slapped him," she said. "How hard?"

"Hurt my hand," I said.

"Guess I won't hit him in that case."

"Let's tackle this issue first," Virgil said. "Maniac, Ranger may have been under the influence of one of the gods popping in to see if they could get Meg to wander off."

"I wouldn't—" I protested, but at the four matching looks I got, I shut my mouth.

"You guys keep trying to give me an excuse, but I'm not taking it," Ranger said.

"We will table the motivation discussion for another time," Virgil said. "The more important issue at hand is that the client who put the contract out on Mirage has put out another one, for twice as much, on Meg."

"Who did you piss off?" Maniac asked.

"I don't know," I said. "I haven't even officially been doing this for a year yet."

It's been one whirlwind of a year for me.

"Where is Mirage?" Greg asked.

Virgil waved behind him at the security screens. "Panic room. I wanted confirmation from Poltergeist that he was considered dead before I sent him on his merry way."

"Keep him there until we get the client out of the way."

"You think he would weasel out of payment?"

"Villain."

"Should we all be aware of company finances?" Ranger

asked.

Virgil paused, his hand at his chin again as he thought about it. "I suppose if we do expand into something larger, you four are the originals and would be members of the board."

"Members of the board?" Ranger said, smirking. "Look at me, ma, I'm a bona fide businessman?"

"Why all the floors if you're not planning on expanding in the first place?" Maniac asked.

"I like to keep my options open," Virgil said.

"Future plans aside," Greg said, "we have more urgent matters."

"That's not new," Maniac said. "There's always more urgent matters."

Ranger was waving a hand at us. "Shush."

"Don't shush us," Maniac said. "The adults are talking."

"I can't hear it!" Ranger said, "You need to," he paused, his head tilted, eyes blank. He hissed in a breath, "Fuck, that's –" he snapped back, looked at us.

"That's what?" Greg asked.

"A lot of blood," Ranger said. "Thought I was watching *Blade* for a second."

"Why do you guys watch that shit for movie night?" I asked. "You don't get enough of it during missions?"

Yes, we have movie nights. We've been having them once a week since we went camping, another part of Ranger's team building exercises. I end up covering my eyes during a lot of the movies they pick. Am I the only one with taste?

"Is it coming in clearly?" Greg asked.

"No," Ranger said. "I'm getting flashes of," his head tilted again, "a bar, shots lined up, the –" he snapped back to us again. "I know that club!"

"When?" Virgil asked.

Ranger frowned, tilting his head again. "After dark, but they won't show up if we're there too early."

"The monsters?" I asked.

"Yes."

"Can you see what they look like?"

"No, just the impression of claws and teeth?" he said, like he wasn't sure. "There's a lot of people in the club, and it doesn't really get hopping until around 11:00."

Virgil checked the time. "It's just past 7:30 now. We should go rest and head over there by – would 10:30 be safe enough to keep them from avoiding it? We'll need to locate and take them out quickly so they don't eat the patrons."

Ranger's eyes were blank again. "Yes, that should be okay."

"Good. Go, eat, rest – whatever you need to do to be ready. Meet me at the Hummer by 10:15."

∞

Ranger was not kidding. There were people lined up to get inside the club stretching back along the block.

I learned something new: club attire is skimpy, for everyone. I would not want to wear that in this weather. How is everyone not freezing? Do they even wear clothes like that in the winter when it's like twenty degrees out with snow on the sidewalks?

Virgil parked the Hummer at the curb by the entrance. The bouncer, a large, muscular man in a skintight black t-shirt, at the outside ropes was trying to tell us we couldn't park there until Virgil spoke to him. "Yes, we can."

"Yes, you can," the bouncer repeated.

"These aren't the droids you're looking for," I muttered. Ranger and Greg heard me and snorted. If Virgil heard me, he ignored it. Maniac had gone ahead and was already pushing her way past a second, similarly attired bouncer at the door. He was trying to argue with her that she couldn't cut the line but stopped when Virgil and the rest of us got up to him.

"Do the hand thing," I said. Virgil looked back at me. "With the mind trick."

"I'm going to revoke your movie night rights," he said,

turning back to the bouncer. "We did wait in line, it's our turn." The bouncer moved out of our way.

Ranger was leading the way because he was the one who knew the club, but the only thing he had seen was when the blood started flying over by the bar. It was set down, back against a wall at one side of the club, and we were hurrying past tables, chairs, and couches. The seating was covered in that vinyl fabric meant to make cleaning up spills easy. Waitresses were having to dodge around us. I could see a dance floor and DJ booth up ahead. It was crowded, and there were a lot of strobing lights in that direction.

We had almost reached the bar when a jovial voice called out, ringing even over the din of the techno music, the yelling chatter of club goers, and the stomp of hundreds of feet. Greg heard him first; he had come to a sudden stop, snagging Ranger by his jacket and putting an arm in my way. Virgil and Maniac had ended up behind us, and they came to a standstill at my back.

"Megaera!" boomed the voice, and Bacchus was striding up to the five of us, his face flushed, his ever-present bottle of whiskey in one hand. He was grinning, a group of men back at the bar howling with laughter and calling him back. "We're about to do shots. Join us!"

"Can't," I said. "Mortal business."

"You can, and you will! Guardian, I will drink you under the table!" He was cheerful, seemingly unbothered by my initial rejection. "All your mortals should come have a shot." He slapped a hand down on Greg's shoulder, and I saw the way Greg tensed, his feet shifting. The way his hands moved, he was ready to take Bacchus down physically, but Bacchus had pulled his own hand away and was shaking it. "What is your Guardian made of?"

I opened my mouth to answer, but Bacchus waved it away. "Doesn't matter. Come." He threw an arm around Greg's shoulder and tried to lead him toward the bar. Greg didn't shift. Bacchus did that awkward step forward and back to catch his balance that you do when you encounter an immovable object you thought was way lighter than it is. He tried to shift Greg again.

Bacchus' face lit up. "Tough customer!" He shoved his bottle of whiskey into Ranger's hands, stepped behind Greg, set both his hands on Greg's back, and tried to push him forward.

The men at the bar were still howling, cheering Bacchus on, then taunting and jeering as it became more obvious that Greg wasn't going anywhere.

Bacchus ended up setting his shoulder against Greg's back, pushing into him like he was one of those dummies they use for blocking practice in football. He still couldn't shift Greg from his spot.

He stepped back, considering, still smiling as he looked the five of us over. "Well then, I'll just bring the shots to you." He headed back to the bar, surprisingly quick and light on his feet, and collected shots from the bartender, who shouted after him, his hands up in that universal "what the fuck?" way.

Guess Bacchus took someone else's order.

He was back over at us and held a shot out to me. "Megaera, you first."

"I don't drink," I said.

He gave the shot a little wiggle, the look in his eyes hardening. "A gift, if you must insist on being stubborn."

Greg plucked the shot from his hand, threw it back, and held the glass back out to Bacchus.

Bacchus laughed. "Yes! Guardian, we will party! But first," he was shoving the shot glasses into everyone else's hands and threw back the extra one he now held since Greg had taken the one meant for me, dumped the two glasses on a nearby table, and held out his now free hands to me. "Come dance with me."

"Can't," I said. "Two left feet."

"That doesn't matter," Bacchus said, "dance is about expression."

"You sound like a muse."

"I have spent some time among them."

The music blasting into the air was giving me a headache, and I could see Greg's jaw was clenched. The level of noise in here was incredible.

Virgil was up at our side, one hand on my arm. "We're wasting time. Meg, you need to get to the back of the club and start clearing people toward the exits."

"What if they stampede?" I asked.

"Try to—" Virgil said, but suddenly we could hear screaming. It rose up above the music, and the bartenders were frantically scrambling over the bar, a tinkling smash of glass as the shelving of liquor bottles came crashing down.

I saw the first of them as it hooked its talons into the person closest to it.

Humanoid in appearance, their skin was a ghastly shade of white, that pale fish-belly color of creatures that live below the surface out of the sun. They had arms, legs, and heads, and they were clothed only in loincloths. If it hadn't been for the single eye set in their face, they could've easily covered anything else that made them stand out as not human.

Cyclopes were supposed to be giants, but that was the only name I could think of to fit what these were.

Bacchus saw what was happening, snatched his bottle of whiskey back from Ranger, and vanished without another word.

Ass.

The Cyclopes moved quickly, swarming out from the bar. I wasn't even sure where they'd come from.

Have you ever seen *28 Days Later*? The jerky, rushing movements the zombies make as they surge toward their prey? How fast they are?

This is why I don't watch horror movies; I practically live one.

People were screaming, and the Cyclopes had fallen on the person they had caught. Greg raced in, slamming into the Cyclopes, trying to pull them off without harming the man underneath the pile.

The people on the dance floor, at the tables, thronging the club had caught wind that something was very, very wrong. Maniac ran forward and blasted the teeming pack of Cyclopes with flames.

Evacuation was not going to be needed, so I called to the whispers. They, the figures and shadows boiled forward, swirling around me. The whispers were howling, the figures already slashing out with their long fingers as the shadows rose around us. One of the Cyclopes knocked Ranger back, into the circle of my power, and then screamed, wailing as the figures and shadows got a hold of him and tore him apart.

It took them a minute to get through his skin because it was tough, leather-like in texture.

Ranger staggered to his feet and swore. "I forgot my bat."

"Is it in the Hummer?" I asked him. "We could go back for it once people are all cleared out." The two of us were backing toward the doors, the figures flowing around us, a barrier between the panicked horde trying to exit and the Cyclopes charging at us.

They had bred themselves an army.

Okay, maybe not quite that large, but there were a lot of them, and calling them a flock doesn't have the same ring to it. They definitely looked like they were equal to the number of zombie rats we found in the warehouse when the Rat King tried to escape.

Ranger grabbed a forgotten bottle of champagne off one of the tables. "I might just have to make do."

The ones charging us hit the edge of my range, and the figures and shadows converged on them. The figures' fingers tore their skin off in strips, as the shadows boiled over and crashed onto them, the Cyclopes screamed, gouging out chunks of their own flesh. When the whispers screamed, they began turning on each other, snarling and ripping with their talons and teeth.

Ranger was watching. "You know, you're making me

feel superfluous right now."

I was on the tips of my toes; I could see Maniac surrounded by flames, part of the bar lit up. Greg was under a massive pile of bodies.

"Where's Virgil?" I said, just as several Cyclopes came flying. They landed on the floor in my perimeter and didn't get the chance to get to their feet, as the figures came spinning back and slammed into them.

"He's over there," Ranger said, pointing.

"Thanks, got that."

Greg shot up into the rafters, shedding Cyclopes. They were trying to dig the talons into his flesh but couldn't, so they slipped off, shrieking when they tumbled down and hit the concrete floor. Then Greg went straight back down, so that he crashed bodily into them, the floor shaking under our feet.

But the Cyclopes he had just crushed weren't getting back up from that.

Behind us, the doors had cleared out, and Ranger and I backed up enough that the doors themselves were blocked by the figures and shadows. They were eddying in the air, rippling as they circled us.

Ranger chucked the champagne bottle at the head of one of the Cyclopes. It was a bullseye, literally, because the heavy bottom hit the thing square in the face. It screamed and fell back. Then he dodged out the door behind us, and was back, bat in hand.

"What's the plan, Stan?" he asked me.

"Containment. Bring them to me so I can make sure they don't get into the street."

"There are other emergency exits."

"They seem too focused on trying to eat us to be looking for those right now."

"You have a point," Ranger said, and he ran out of the protection the figures and shadows afforded him, attracting the attention of the Cyclopes who had been streaming in past the burning bar. The ones who made it through without getting crisped by Maniac had continued their charge into the room, settling on heading for Greg, who was crushing their heads like sparrows' eggs, or heading for Virgil who was keeping them back off him with one hand while sweeping groups of them into Maniac's flames or my circle of shadows with the other.

At this point they didn't want to get near me until Ranger slammed the bat into the head of the one nearest. It staggered, turning with a growl, and Ranger hit it again. The growl turned into a shriek that got the others near it to turn, and as a group, they leapt at Ranger, who peddled back from them, dodging as he got twisted around to run back to me.

He slipped in the blood surrounding me and went down, rolled so that the figures and shadows billowed over him, and they snagged the Cyclopes that had followed him. The creatures screamed as the figures burrowed their fingers in and dragged them further into the circle so that the Cyclopes were caught, screeching as they flailed.

Ranger hurriedly got out of the way and got back next to me. His jacket was streaked with blood, and he took a moment to examine it. "Damn, between getting shot and now this, I think this one is finished." He sounded sad about it.

"That's why I won't wear my good jacket to this kind of event."

"At least you're wearing the one I gave Greg."

"He glared at me until I put it on."

"You're that upset at me—" he protested.

"No," I said, interrupting him. "I am not having this conversation *now*. I am not discussing my survival instincts literally in the middle of a mission."

I could've had the conversation. I wasn't having to pay a whole lot of attention because we were at the point where Virgil was just soft balling the Cyclopes into the figures and shadows a couple at a time so they could rip them apart. Maniac was finishing up her barbecue station, and Greg had spread several more of them in bloody smears across the floor.

"Your survival instincts cannot be that—"

"Yes, yes, they are."

The Cyclopes were dead, piles of torn and crushed bodies, entrails. The floor slick with blood was all that remained at this point.

That was when the fire suppression system decided to go off. The sprinklers turned on, soaking all of us, and putting out what was left of Maniac's flames.

There was a collective sigh from the five of us, and the whispers laughed.

"Meg?" Greg called, but the whispers, figures, and shadows had already curled their way over to me and faded, brushing my face with their fingers as they went.

Ranger and I headed over in his direction, and Greg fell into step with us. His clothes were soaked with blood and water, dripping off him in pinkish trails. He had to push his hair out of his face.

We joined Maniac and Virgil over at the bar. Virgil had climbed over the counter and was examining the area.

"Where did they come in from?" Greg asked.

Maniac had snagged a bottle of grenadine off the floor and was drinking it.

"What are you doing?" Ranger asked.

"It's sugar syrup," she said. "I need the energy."

"Glad you know that because I didn't want to be the one to point out it's got no alcohol."

Maniac snorted. "I don't do shots while I'm working, unlike some people apparently."

Virgil crouched down behind the bar, and I leaned onto it to peer over. He was looking down a man-sized hole in the floor. Whatever grate had been covering it was gone. Greg leaned over the bar next to me.

"Don't get that on me," I said absently.

The sprinklers were still going, so when I turned my head to look at him, he had water trickling down his face. He was smiling at me. "What?" I asked.

"I like doing these kinds of missions with you."

"You cannot tell me you have a good time doing this," I said, but I was smiling back.

"I do when people aren't shooting at you."

"Maniac," Virgil called, "come light this up."

Maniac hopped over the bar, looked down into the hole in the floor, and held out a hand. Flames flared out, down into the space. There were surprised screams and shrieks, the scrabbling of talons against concrete.

"Don't think they're all dead yet," Ranger said.

Greg wasn't smiling anymore. He went over the bar to join Virgil and Maniac, who had stopped sending flames down. Smoke was drifting up out of it. "Who's going in first?" he asked.

"I am," I said, coming over the bar. I saw Greg taking a breath to argue, so I beat him to it. "They'll clear back from me, and you can send Ranger in right after me if you need to."

"Meg can follow where they go and lead us to their nest," Virgil said.

I didn't wait for anything more. I pulled the whispers back to me, and they, the figures, the shadows and I slid into the hole in the floor and dropped. I heard Greg make a startled, strangled noise because I hadn't waited for anyone to help me down there, and I had moved quickly enough that everyone was still gathered at the top.

I landed on top of a body, and staggered back, hitting the wall. The Cyclops my feet had stumbled over wasn't totally dead yet; it rose with a pained wail, because its skin was charred, slipping off the pink muscle beneath. The whispers wailed back, the figures and shadows slamming into it so that it hit the floor of the tunnel I was in and tore into it.

There was a chittering, a scrambling noise farther up the tunnel, and I turned to face it. I looked up, the other four peering down the hole, so I pointed ahead of me. "I'm going this way."

"Meg, wait!" Ranger was slipping his way in, and I stepped forward so that he landed behind me. "Don't just run off without back-up!"

"It's just Cyclopes."

"Gods. What if they decide to show up while you're off too far ahead of us?"

The whispers and I paused because he had a point. But there was only one god whose intentions for us alone we were worried about. We might not know Poseidon's cost, but we knew it had to be a better alternative than whatever Zeus had planned.

I let the figures and shadows out far enough that Ranger was in our circle and stepped forward, down the tunnel. Behind us, I heard feet hit the concrete as Greg, Maniac and Virgil followed us down the hole and then down the tunnel. Ranger pulled out his phone, using the flashlight on it so everyone could see where they were going.

I didn't need it. I was following the tug of the whispers, my feet sure on the flat surface, and I could hear the scraping and scrabbling still ahead as the Cyclopes pulled back from us. The figures and shadows went sweeping along ahead of me and snagged one, ripping into it and leaving its still-twitching body for Ranger and me to step over.

"I would not want to be on your bad side," Ranger said.

"How do you know you aren't?" I asked.

"He's on my bad side," Maniac called up.

I heard Greg chuckle.

"Glad I'm the team joke now," Ranger said.

"You're not," I said, "it's like the time Virgil wrecked."

Virgil sighed.

I had to stop because I had come to a ledge. I hadn't been paying attention to the whispers, who swirled around me right before I went over it Ranger made a wild grab, snagging my arm and waist and pulling me back, and then he snatched his hands away like he had burnt them.

He cleared his throat, "Sorry."

I turned my head to look at him, and he ducked his face away. "Why?" we asked.

He ignored the question, raising his phone. He had managed not to drop it when he pulled us back, and now the light fell over the teeming mass of bodies at the bottom of the well that the Cyclopes had dug out.

"That's a lot of heartbeats," Greg said from the back, "how many are there?"

"Doesn't matter," we said, and we slipped past Ranger's grasp, sliding down the exposed dirt, sending clods and bits of leftover concrete flying.

"Damn it, Meg!" I heard the two of them say at the same time.

We hit the bottom, and the shadows crashed down onto the Cyclopes at the floor who hadn't cleared back in time to avoid us. The figures swirled up around me, the wind they made ruffling my hair, and then they flowed forward, reaching with their fingers as we glided toward the gibbering mass, who tried to flee from us, but the heroes were blocking their only door.

There were gouts of blood spraying as the figures and shadows eddied in the air, boiling and swarming the horde of Cyclopes, who were stuck, running in circles, because any time they tried to head for the tunnel Maniac lit them up. Virgil was leaning out, carefully placed at the edge of the ledge, snagging Cyclops and tossing them into the figures and shadows as they backed away from me.

The whispers were howling and laughing, and every Cyclopes they brushed by turned on its comrade so that they were tearing at each other and themselves as often as the figures were ripping into them.

The ground beneath our feet rumbled. Surprised, we took a step toward the doorway, but at this point we had worked our way around, so we were all the way across the dug-out room from the exit.

Something emerged from the floor, and now I could see why there were tales of the Cyclopes as giants. He was massive, shedding dirt and rock as he shook himself free, and the roar issuing from his mouth made the space around us vibrate. Talon claws, fish-belly white, he rose up, and up, a single blinking, rolling eye in the center of his face.

He spotted us and raised one enormous fist.

The whispers had not expected this.

"Oh, fuck," I said, as the fist started downwards, and I turned to duck and run.

The giant Cyclops roared again, this time in surprise and pain as Greg slammed into it, knocking it back into a wall, and the space around us shook again, dirt raining down from the ceiling.

"Infrastructure!" Virgil yelled.

"I fucking know!" Greg yelled back, I heard the crunch of bone as he hit the thing in the jaw, but it grabbed him in that immense hand and threw him.

He hit the wall on the other side, the room shaking again.

"Damn it!" Virgil was yelling, "Don't bring the building down on us!"

"Tell him that!" Greg shot back, from the him-shaped hole he was climbing out of.

The whispers, figures, shadows and I were busy running around the edge of the room toward the door because I did not want to end up under that thing's feet.

The giant Cyclops staggered, its feet making the ground quake under mine, and it snarled, because Greg had slammed into it again, but this time its hands were headed for the doorway, and Virgil, Maniac and Ranger were crowded at the edge.

The men's hands were up, and the creature slowed, then stuttered to a stop. Maniac's hands came out, and then flames were streaming. The thing bellowed, it's leathery skin blackening, but the flames just licked up it, leaving only scorches.

"Oh, that's not good," Maniac said. "Hey, guys, this thing might be fireproof."

Greg slammed into it yet again; this time, when it staggered, it fell to the ground, and the impact as it landed knocked my feet out from under me.

I was staring at it's one, mammoth eye, and its mouth opened, revealing broad, shovel like teeth, as it roared again.

Its breath smelled like rotten flesh, and I gagged, scrambling backwards, because it was reaching for me again. The whispers screamed, figures and shadows spinning forward, slashing, and it howled, snatching its hand back, melon sized droplets of blood splashing down.

Greg landed on it, and was hammering a fist repeatedly into its chest, I could hear the ribs cracking, and the Cyclops shrieked; the booming, high pitched noise it emitted made me cover my ears, although that didn't help.

Greg stumbled back, his own ears covered. "Son of a—" he started, but he didn't finish because one of the flailing arms hit him, and he went bouncing over the ground, hitting the wall at the other end.

The Cyclops had stopped shrieking at least. It was climbing to its feet, and I could see the collapsed section of its chest where Greg had almost broken through the ribs. It turned to face me, and roared again, half bent at the waist, a shudder working its way down its head and shoulders, like a bull ready to charge.

The figures and shadows swirled up around me, swaying and circling; we waited while the whispers screamed their challenge.

The Cyclops charged us.

One gigantic foot hit the edge of my range, and the figures dug their fingers in long furrows down the bottom of the sole, tearing slices deep into the flesh.

It shrieked again, bellowing in surprise, then screamed again when it stepped down on the injured foot; it fell to the side, and the whispers, figures, shadows and I had to dodge out of the way or get crushed under it.

As it was, one of the hands knocked my legs out from

under me, and I hit the ground hard, my breath gone. I saw the palm hovering over me, and I curled into a ball, instinctively covering my head. The figures slashed again, droplets of blood raining down on us, and then I went sliding across the dirt toward the doorway. I stopped at the bottom of the wall.

"Meg!" Virgil was yelling, "Get *up!*"

I needed my brain to catch up to what just happened before I could get my limbs to cooperate.

Fortunately for me, Greg had recovered, and Virgil and Ranger were keeping the Cyclops back, Ranger slowing it so Virgil could shove it toward the wall on the other side of the room. Greg came up and hit it head on, right in the spot where he had caved the ribs.

There was a nasty, squelching, crunching noise when he hit it, and the Cyclops made a kind of surprised squeaking squeal. It staggered further back, hitting the wall, and the roof of dirt and concrete above shook again. With another squishing noise, Greg set his feet against the side of the Cyclops, and ripped himself free, dragging a heart out with him. He hauled it backwards, snarling, and the arteries tore, blood spraying into the air.

The Cyclops collapsed, and Greg landed on the dirt floor on his back, the heart landing by him with a wet thud, his top half absolutely soaked in the gore. He was clawing the blood out of his eyes, and then rolled onto his side, retching.

I think at that moment all of us were on our knees trying not to vomit, because the stench in the air was horrendous. It smelled like someone had mixed together a bucket of rotting fish and cow offal and then thrown it in a latrine.

"Fuck," Ranger said from above me.

"Meg," Virgil said, his voice sounding strained, "can you let them go so I can get you up here? I don't think any of us want to smell this any longer than we have to."

Greg had gotten to his feet and pulled his shirt off; he was using the inside of it to get as much of the remaining blood off his face, arms, hands and hair as possible. It was spattered on his shoes and jeans, and he was looking at them, brow furrowed.

I was looking at my own clothes, spattered in the same blood. "My jacket got ruined."

"Meg," Virgil repeated.

"I've got her," Greg said. "We're both covered in this shit anyway." I let the whispers go, and he was striding up to me, kneeling on the ground, his ear pressed to my stomach, fingers gently flexing against my thighs. He sighed, "I love the sound they make together."

"You know eventually he's going to be out of there, right?" I said teasingly.

He stood up, "But you'll both be in the same room at times, so I'll still get to hear them beating together."

"How do you manage to be so sickeningly cute together?" Maniac called down. "You're giving me cavities."

CHAPTER FOURTEEN

When we got back up to the club, the sprinklers had stopped because the police and fire department had arrived.

Someone somehow had managed to call the National Guard, who had apparently put them in touch with *that* branch of the military, so a hero was waiting for us topside.

"Striker," Greg said, sounding pleasantly surprised.

Striker was a leanly muscled black man, his long hair in locs hanging loosely around his face. He, unlike Greg, who hadn't worn his hero suit even when he was military, was clothed in a tight fitting, electric blue, tactical armor-style suit.

"Fortress," Striker said, "fancy meeting you here. Freelancing going well?"

"Well enough," Greg said.

Striker was looking the five of us over, "Looks like your team is full up. Didn't want to save me a spot?"

"I've currently got room for more," Virgil said, "and you're at the top of a very short list of preferreds."

Striker smiled, revealing very even, white teeth. Unlike some people, he still looked friendly baring his teeth that way. "Good to know. Who else is on it? Please tell me BulletProof didn't make the cut."

"Perish the thought that I would let that idiot on my team," Virgil muttered, then more loudly, "I was thinking of extending an invitation to Poltergeist if they're amenable to quitting mercenary work."

"I'd be willing to work with them," Striker said, "Mind introducing me to the rest of your team?"

Virgil waved a hand at us, "Ranger, Maniac and Vengeance."

Striker's eyes lit up. "Vengeance?" he reached a hand out toward me, and I took it. His grip was firm, warm as he shook my hand. "Nice to finally meet you."

"Ditto," I said.

"Fortress tell you all about me?"

"Nope."

"Seriously?" Striker said, "You don't tell your girl anything about your friends?"

"Nope," I said. "So, I'm going to need to hear—"

Greg cleared his throat, snagging me around the waist. "The subject hasn't come up much."

Striker clicked his tongue, "Dude, he used to get up to all kinds of shit with us. Then he and Patrice broke up, and she left him with that table—"

Greg was making slashing movements over his throat, and I nudged him, "Quit it. I wanna hear this."

"Yeah, Fortress," said Ranger, smirking, "we wanna hear this."

Greg turned to glare at Ranger, who gazed back at him, still smirking.

"What was that, like, three or four years ago?" Striker said.

Around the same time that Poltergeist had last gone drinking with Greg. "Bad breakup?" I asked innocently.

Greg turned his glare to me, "Not that kind of bad."

"He got all serious," Striker said, "when she turned. Wouldn't go out anymore. I mean, he was already living, breathing, and sleeping the hero life, but that killed his fun side."

"As fascinating as this must be for Ranger, I'm afraid we

need to be getting back to headquarters. Striker, you have my number. Call me when your contract is up," Virgil said, herding us toward the door. Greg was using the hand on my waist to gently steer me away from Striker, while I was trying to lean around him to shoot questions in his direction.

"How much was that stupid table?" I yelled back, but Striker just waved a hand and turned back toward the officers trying to catch his attention, while Greg, Virgil, Ranger and Maniac were all working to keep me marching by the cops trying to get us to stop and tell them what had happened.

Outside the club doors, standing among the flashing, strobing lights of the fire trucks, ambulances and police cars, there were still a lot of club goers gathered around, most of them huddled under those shiny thermal blankets for emergencies. The paramedics were moving among them, checking vital signs and pupils, and I assume discussing who if any of them needed transport to a hospital.

"Hey! Hey!" someone yelled, and then Susan and her cameraman skidded to a stop next to us, "I've got questions for you..." her eyes trailed down, because Greg was still shirtless, and she had focused on his chest.

"Susan," Virgil said, drawing her attention up to his face, "to what do we owe the pleasure?"

She flushed, tearing her eyes away from Virgil's face to focus on the sidewalk for a minute before she squared her shoulders and looked him in the eyes. "What happened? The clubbers are talking about one-eyed monsters trying to eat someone."

"There were, in fact, one-eyed monsters," Virgil said smoothly.

The cameraman was recording, his camera set on his shoulder.

"Why is Fortress shirtless? Were you here to—"

"No," Greg said. "We were not here to party. If you'll excuse us," he scooped me up, "Vengeance and I have places to be. Vigilante, we'll see you back at the Tower."

He took off, leaving the other three to deal with Susan and her cameraman.

∞

He landed us on our balcony, doing that new pause of his where he listens at the door before he let me go in. Then he steered me over to the bathroom and got the shower started.

Our shower – and I assume Virgil's, Ranger's and Maniac's – is set up specifically to get blood, bone and other bits of gore washed off. The drain even has a special trap for catching things so they don't end up in the plumbing.

Our own little slaughterhouse shower.

Okay, ours is large enough for two people to comfortably shower together. I don't know about the others, but maybe Virgil planned ahead for that; he's done it for almost everything else.

There's even a special trash chute in the bathroom for the clothes that aren't salvageable.

It sees a lot of use.

Greg looked over my jacket. He pulled down the zipper, slid it off my arms, held it up to examine it, and sighed. "Yeah, this one is fucked."

He tossed it into the shoot without another glance. His shoes, his jeans, my shoes, my jeans, and then my clean shirt met the same fate.

"Hey!" I said, "That one was fine!"

"Damn it, sorry, autopilot," Greg said. He was washing the dried streaks of blood off his hands and arms; they were still damp when he went for the zipper on my latest catsuit.

His lips hovered over the back of my neck as he was peeling it down, and then he reared back.

"What?" I asked, twisting to try and figure out what had happened.

"That stuff is in your hair," he said, his face looking green. "It smells awful."

"Oh gross," I said, speeding up to get the suit off. He helped me get it peeled the rest of the way off, and then I practically leapt into the water. I was standing under one showerhead, hanging my head upside down under the other, running my fingers through my curls to try and pull the blood out.

He joined me, snagging my shampoo and helping me get it washed out.

It took us a while to get all the blood off, because that stuff gets into all kinds of places. I was finding streaks of it on my neck, and it had managed to leak under the suit and leave trails down my chest.

Greg was covered in smears of it everywhere other than his hands and arms at this point.

It took a surprising amount of time for the water to finally run clear. There's a reason Virgil set each apartment up with tankless water heaters.

By the time we were clean and dry, all I wanted to do was lie down, so I ended up grabbing clean underwear and pajamas from our drawers and climbing into our bed. Greg had halfheartedly protested, but gave up. He sent Virgil a text to let him know which apartment we were in and then climbed in next to me, pulling me against his chest and curling around me.

∞

There was a crib in the middle of the apartment, situated halfway between the bedroom and the living room.

I could hear a baby crying, the wail emanating from the crib, and I wanted desperately to help, but I couldn't step forward because someone was already there, leaning over the railings, crooning a lullaby in a language I knew but couldn't remember.

She looked up at me and smiled, her eyes as cold and blue as they had been on the shore of the lake, her hair pulled back in a chignon bun, the drum-like rattle of her Guardian's tail in her voice as she sang.

She reached into the crib to take him.

∞

I sat up, the whispers howling in my ears.

Never, they said.

There was a thud that shook the floor under the bed, and the whispers vanished.

"God damn it," Greg said, and then he had come back over the edge of the bed. "Meg, are you okay?"

"Nightmare," I said, my heartbeat slowing. At least it hadn't been another dream about Red Eye.

Is it normal that I would rather deal with Hera than with another Red Eye? I don't know that I should find her less frightening than him.

Greg settled next to me, pulling me back against him, his nose in my hair as he kissed the top of my head. "Short one at least?"

"Yes," I said. I wasn't going back to sleep, though, there was sunlight streaming in through our windows. "Did everyone make it back okay?"

"As far as I know."

"What was the thud?"

"I rolled off the bed when they came out."

"You fell off the bed?" I asked, grinning at him.

"Rolled. It was intentional."

"Uh huh," I said, "sure you did."

He had one hand on my chin, gently tilting my face up to his, "It was absolutely, completely intentional," he said, lowering his lips to mine.

I kissed him back, twining my arms around his neck. He was slipping his hands up under my shirt, his fingers just grazing the skin, and I shivered.

His phone rang, and he pulled back with a swear, leaning around me to pick it up. I could feel the tension of his body change, and when he answered the phone, I knew why.

"Poltergeist," he said, "where are you?"

Whatever Poltergeist's answer was, it made Greg let go of me and scoot off the bed to pace alongside the windows and the balcony door.

I sighed and got up, headed over to the kitchen, and started pulling out the coffee beans and grinder. While the beans were grinding, I got the water reservoir for the pot filled and stuck in a paper filter, beans in, hit the brew now button.

I turned and checked the fridge for any food items that had been left in it when we changed apartments, then sighed again because Greg had cleared it out. We were going to have to trek downstairs or go out.

Greg had stopped pacing and was standing at the window, one hand in his hair, "Did she say why she had put a contract out on Vengeance?" He paused, listening, "No, no we can't give it that long, someone already took the contract. Last night, right after you called me."

"Poltergeist's client is a woman?" I asked. Greg nodded and waved me off because he was still listening.

"Yeah, thanks. Call me when you're in town and we'll get your other contract done." Greg hung up and was texting as he made his way over to me.

"So, who is it?" I asked. He looked up from his phone to answer me, and his face paled.

I turned to look behind me, thinking something had popped up in the apartment, but the kitchen was empty, and I turned back toward him to ask what would make him look that way when I got my answer.

Greg had heard it before we felt it, and had he not already been moving towards me when it hit, I might have died in that moment.

The building rumbled. At first it was a small vibration, and then between one breath and the next the whole thing shuddered beneath my feet. The ceiling collapsed and the floor crumbled away beneath me as the quake heaved the building upward. Greg leapt forward, tackling me, and we hit a piece of the floor that had cracked, tilting itself backward, twisting and rolling down it to hit the wall over in the dining area. Then he let go of me, surging upwards, catching the slab that had plummeted from above our heads, bracing it across his shoulders, neck and back as he knelt over me.

"Meg! Stay under me!"

I could see the strain across his muscles, as more of the concrete above us groaned and gave way under the strain of the rolling earth, dipping and swaying in a way it had no right to. I did as he ordered, cowering up against him, my shoulder pressed into his chest, my hands pressed to his thigh, his breath harsh in my ear and against the back of my neck.

In front of us, the shattering concrete seemed to slow, floating in the air, and I thought Ranger must have made his way to us. Until the sea swept in, and he came striding with it, dark hair wet and straggling as always. I turned my head, and his eyes caught mine. They had changed, the dark green of them spilling out, swirling along his brow and cheeks. The water came rushing from all sides, slamming into us, and it grabbed on to me, forcibly dragging me away from Greg as it knocked my legs out from under me. My shoulder hit the floor, the water in my face, and I choked, gasping because I had taken a surprised breath and breathed in ocean rather than air.

Greg had let go of the sides of the slab, desperately reaching for me, my own arms extended, but the waves slid me from his grasp. The last touch we shared was when his fingers brushed mine before Poseidon's arms banded around me, and the sea twisted around us, spraying up into the air.

We vanished, Greg's howl following me into darkness.

∞

When I woke, I was on a beach with Poseidon again, staring at the sky above. My head felt fuzzy, blurry and full of buzzing.

"You're awake," Poseidon said from his seated position on the sand beside me. "I miscalculated. I didn't realize your fragility would mean you shouldn't travel in our customary way."

I groaned, "So you owe me now, right?" I was wrung out, somehow still damp and yet parched.

"You came back to yourself on your own, so your debt has not increased," he said, then added thoughtfully, "although perhaps you would owe a new one to Hades otherwise."

"Great. Good to know I've got that going for me." I still hadn't tried to sit up, because I was afraid of what would happen if I did. My mind kept wandering. There was something important I needed to remember, and when it finally worked its way through, I sat up too quickly, and my stomach rolled with my movement. I pitched to the side onto my hands and knees, panting, eyes shut, waiting for the roiling nausea to pass.

There was a cool hand on my back and Poseidon's voice in my ear, deep and rolling like the sea. "Hera's blessing is intact."

"Why do you care?" I said, too angry now to be careful.

"I risk a great deal keeping you in debt to me. Even more bringing you here, as a guest."

"Your toxic family dynamics are not my problem."

"But your interference is."

"What of yours could I possibly be interfering with?" I snapped.

He was silent, and I wasn't sure if I had offended him. In that moment I wasn't sure if I cared.

"I have need of your Guardian," he said eventually.

"Why?"

"My business is my own."

"I'm not even going to consider loaning him to you until you tell me what it's for," I snarled.

"Then I suppose you'll remain my guest until you reconsider."

"How long was I out for?" I asked, switching topics.

"Only a day."

Not that long then. But Greg must be frantic, and I had no way of knowing if the others were okay.

"How many people died in that earthquake you hit us with?"

Poseidon shrugged, "Not my concern."

"Well, it's a concern for me!"

"Your love for them is a weakness, and there are those among us who would exploit that."

"Like you're not already doing that," I muttered.

"I'm not. I'm exploiting their love for you."

I glared at him.

"He will come for you, and he will bargain, and unlike you, he will have no qualms giving me what I want," Poseidon said confidently.

"Yes, he will." Greg wouldn't risk others.

"Your certainty in him is amusing, but every mortal has a price, and I know his."

That gave me pause. Virgil had said guilt would only hold Greg back so far when it came to our baby and me. I had to consider the question that had already been there: would he compromise everything he was if it would keep us safe?

"Were the theatrics entirely necessary?" I asked.

"He needed sufficient motivation."

"Why can't I just perform whatever task it is you want him for?"

He was looking down his nose at me again, "Hera's blessing. Surely you won't risk your one protection against my brother for your Guardian's sake?"

I clenched my jaw because he had me there. If something happened to our child because I chose a stupid move like that, Greg would never forgive me. I don't know that I would be able to forgive myself. Hero work against monsters was one thing, but to risk him to keep Greg from having to take on my debt? Well, even I'm not that misguidedly selfish.

Poseidon stood, not bothering to brush off the sand clinging to his skin, and I averted my face, since he was still going around naked. "When your Guardian comes for you, call me. Don't try to run. Chases are droll." He foamed away, back into the sea, leaving me alone on the beach. How quickly he expected Greg to find me, if at all, out in the middle of nowhere, I wasn't sure.

I stood up. He had taken me while I was still in my pajamas, and the fabric had dried stiff from all the salt water; it made that rustling crunch noise as I moved.

I didn't have any shoes either, and my hair had dried with salt in it, so it was crunchy feeling too.

I swiped at the tears on my face. I was not going to cry about being kidnapped while wearing my pajamas, damn it!

I took a breath and called the whispers to me, and they came, the figures furling around me as the shadows pooled, darkening the white sand. Once I had done that, we took a minute to take stock of our situation. The sea was in front of us, waves crashing on the shore, sheer cliffs to either side of the small, half-moon beach we stood on. Could we leave the cove we were in along the sides of the cliffs?

A short exploration told us no, we couldn't. The cliffs extended out into the water, and the shore dropped off sharply, too deep for us to be able to wade our way around them, and with the waves crashing directly against the stone, there was no way we would survive that experience.

We turned around to check the back of the beach, and there we saw the entrance to a cave, so we headed up the shore and went inside.

The entrance was well past the mark for high tide, but when we went in and ran a hand along the smooth walls, we saw a hole in the ceiling letting in sunlight, shining down on a hole in the floor, and from it we could hear the sea still. We went right up to the edge and peaked down.

Below us, the water swirled and foamed, spraying up at us when it crashed against the rocks. The noise it made echoed up around us, bouncing off the walls until we were surrounded by the swoosh of it, like one giant heartbeat of the earth.

Poseidon had made another mistake. In here, we could hide the beat of our heart. The sound of the sea would drown it out.

∞

It had been three days since I had woken on the beach. The whispers came and went as they pleased; they were as tired of having the sea in their ears as I was.

I couldn't blame them for not hanging around constantly. It was incredibly boring here because nothing changed but the tides.

Well, it's not entirely true that *nothing* was happening. Poseidon was leaving me gifts.

There was a flat rock just outside the entrance to the cave, and so far, each morning when I had come outside to check the horizon for any sign of Greg – partially out of fear he had found me, partially out of hope that if he had I could warn him off before Poseidon realized he was there – I had found a different pearl resting on it.

To date, he had left a cream, chocolate and then a golden colored one.

I had left them on the rock, not even touching them to see if they were real. I wasn't entirely sure why he was leaving them there other than that he had referred to me as his guest, or maybe he was trying to bribe me into cooperation.

The one bringing me food, and a huge pack of water bottles, was Bacchus.

I knew it was him because he had left a bottle of wine with the water and was leaving clusters of grapes with the rest of the food.

I threw the wine and grapes into the hole in the cave floor, and the sea swallowed them up.

I ate the rest of the food he left because I had no other

choice.

But today, I paused over the grapes, considering. I left them on the plate, grabbed a piece of broken shale from the floor of the cave by the entrance, which was littered with them and rocks, and stepped outside.

"Bacchus," I called, and then I waited.

He didn't leave me cooling my heels for long because he appeared next to me, his ever-present bottle of whiskey in one hand. He was already facing me, his eyes wary. "You rang?"

"I have a bargain for you."

"I hate debts—" he said rolling his eyes.

"For a dance?"

He paused, "What are you asking for, and I'll tell you if I'll consider the price."

"Deliver a message for me, to one of my mortals."

"I am not interfering with whatever Poseidon needs your Guardian for."

"Not to him. To the one with the beard, Vigilante."

I saw him weighing it, and he took out his pack of cigarettes, smacking it against his palm as he thought it through. "What's the message?"

I brought the piece of shale up, grabbed a clump of curls, and in one quick motion sliced it through and the lock of hair came loose. I held out the curls to Bacchus, "Tell him we're safe."

I had considered sending my ring, but if Greg saw it, he might get the wrong idea about my message and its intentions, and if he thought I was leaving him to keep him safe, he would only keep searching.

"For a dance?" he asked.

"For a dance," I said.

"At a time and place of my choosing?"

"You hold the debt; you make the rules."

He took the curls, tucked them into a pocket on the inside of his jacket, and slipped the pack of cigarettes in among them. Then his hand caught mine, and he bent over it as he turned it palm up and kissed it. I felt the tingle of his power as it raced up my arm.

"Sealed with a kiss," he said with a wink that reminded me of Ranger, and then he vanished.

∞

When Bacchus came back the next day, he didn't just bring food.

He appeared in the cave, standing next to me, where I was sitting, watching the sea foam and froth in the hole in the floor. It was high tide, and the spray was soaking the wall at the back.

He settled next to me, setting the plate of food aside, and held out a folded pile of clothing with a pair of chucks on top to me.

I took them, confused. "What is this?"

"Your mortal thought you might want clean clothes," he said. "He made me wait until he had suitable attire gathered."

"What was the cost for that?"

"Your Firestarter offered me a night."

I whipped my head around to stare at him, "What?" I asked, angry that he would take that kind of advantage.

He held up a conciliatory palm, "I didn't take the debt. I think she was doing it to irritate – the one who's immune, to irritate him."

I grinned at him, "Not into vengeance-related debts?"

"I would hardly deny you the right to your own calling."

I told you vengeance involves things that are petty. But maybe you don't remember that little speech.

Bacchus waited silently next to me, and I stared him down. With a sigh, he got up. "Prude," he said and vanished.

"Sex offender," I muttered, but he must have truly gone because I don't think he would have been able to help trying to get the last word in edgewise. But he had brought me news I needed: Virgil, Maniac and Ranger were safe enough to have been present when Bacchus showed up.

I got up and moved the food away from the edge, back to the wall where I was keeping the bottles of fresh water, and then I checked over the clothes.

I felt around the inside of the shoes, removing the laces and inspecting everything. I shook out the shirt and turned the socks inside out.

I went over every stitch, including the underwear and bralette, but didn't find anything until I picked up the jeans.

Virgil had slipped a phone into the back pocket, and then folded the jeans up so it was hidden and safely contained, cushioned by the other clothing.

It was off, and I stood there holding it, staring at the blank screen.

Did I dare risk it?

I turned it on, waiting impatiently for it to boot up, and then when it did, almost cried from relief. There was a signal, which meant wherever I was Poseidon had left me close enough to civilization that cell towers were a thing.

I called Virgil, bouncing on the balls of my feet when it connected and then rang.

He picked up almost immediately, "Meg! Where—"

I interrupted him, "Where's the tracker?"

He ignored me, "Meg, where are you?"

I ignored him in return, "Poseidon wants Greg for something. I'm not telling you where I am because you'll tell him. Where's the tracker?"

He didn't get to answer me because I heard the muffled noises of a scuffle, and then Greg's voice was on the line, hoarse, desperate and relieved all at once, "Meg! Meg, sweetheart, where are you?"

His voice in my ear almost crumbled my resolve. I was on my knees, my heart in my throat, my chest constricted; I was down, my forehead resting against the cave floor. My face wet with tears, I had never wanted so badly to be safe in someone's arms.

"I don't know. There's," I croaked, "there's only the sea."

"Meg, I need landmarks, I've been looking for you, but the world's a big place. Please, please, look around. What do you see?" he was pleading.

"I love you," I said.

"Meg don't—" I could hear the alarm in his voice, the panic starting to rise.

I hung up.

I took a moment to sob on the cave floor, and then I staggered to my feet, grabbed a rock from the entrance, and smashed the phone. I searched through the pieces, and there it was, Virgil had hidden the tracker behind the screen. I smashed it too, and then for good measure swept the remnants into the hole in the floor where they were swallowed by the sea.

I grabbed another piece of shale and sliced through the shoes, tearing the soles apart, peeling back the rubber.

Virgil's always had my number. He had hidden two of them in separate spots, one in each shoe.

Those got broken and tossed into the water too.

The whispers were at my back, the figures' fingers resting against my shoulders, curling their way down my arms, the shadows at my feet.

I got back to my feet, padded barefoot, for good now, to the entrance of the cave, and sat down, watching the waves.

There was only the sea, the sand, the whispers, figures, shadows and me.

ABOUT THE AUTHOR

Jamie lives in Charlotte, NC with her husband, three feral children and two badly behaved dogs.

She has BAs in English and Theatre, her favorite part of which was working backstage on traveling Broadway productions.